Charles Frederick Forshaw

The Poets of Spen Valley

Being Biographies and Poems...

Charles Frederick Forshaw

The Poets of Spen Valley
Being Biographies and Poems...

ISBN/EAN: 9783744765176

Printed in Europe, USA, Canada, Australia, Japan

Cover: Foto ©Raphael Reischuk / pixelio.de

More available books at **www.hansebooks.com**

THE POETS

OF THE

Spen Valley.

BEING

BIOGRAPHIES AND POEMS, BY VARIOUS
AUTHORS, OF THE PARLIAMENTARY DIVISION
OF THE SPEN VALLEY.

EDITED BY

CHAS. F. FORSHAW, LL.D.

HONORARY DOCTOR OF DENTAL SURGERY OF THE BALTIMORE
COLLEGE OF DENTAL SURGERY;
EDITOR, "YORKSHIRE POETS, PAST AND PRESENT," YORKSHIRE SONNETTEERS,"
"YORKSHIRE BALLADS," ETC. ETC.

BRADFORD:
PRINTED AND PUBLISHED BY THORNTON AND PEARSON, THE COLLEGE PRESS,
BARKEREND ROAD.

1892.

Illustrations.

STOCKS HAMMOND, Esq. B.A.'

TO

✦ STOCKS HAMMOND, Esq. ✦

B.A. L. Mus.

PRINCIPAL OF THE VICTORIA COLLEGE OF MUSIC;

FELLOW OF THE SOCIETY OF ANTIQUARIES OF SCOTLAND. ETC.

THOU hast the power the subtlest sounds to weave
    Into sweet strains of thrilling harmony ;
Thou hast the will heroic to achieve
    Still doughtier deeds with fitting minstrelsy.
What better tribute could a poet pay
    To one who weds his words to such gay sounds
That steps he lithe and lightsome on his way,
    Whilst his glad heart with winsome laughter bounds ?
Music and song belovèd are by all,
    And thou art powerful to portray their charms :
For Terpsichore is ready at thy call
    To soothe, to thrill, or fill with wild alarms !
So I to thee this volume dedicate
To brighten, beautify, and elevate.

EDITOR.

The following Gentlemen have contributed the Biographical

Sketches of the Authors under notice :—

GEORGE ACKROYD, Esq. J.P.

JOSEPH N. CUTTS. Ph.D. B.Sc.

Dr. P. H. DAVIS, F.R.H.S. F.R.G.S. F.S.A.

ALBERT E. ELLISON, M.D.S.

JOHN FIRTH.

CHAS. F. FORSHAW, LL.D.

JOSEPH GAUNT, B.A.

W. H. HATTON, F.R.H.S.

WALTER J. KAYE, M.A.

Rev. THOMAS KING, M.A.

Rev. B. MAYOU. M.A.

FRANK PEEL.

A. RAMAGE, M.D. L.F.P.S.G.

HERBERT SHACKLETON, M.R.C.S. Eng. L.R.C.P.I.

Rev. JOSEPH STRAUSS. M.A. Ph.D.

J. A. ERSKINE STUART. L.R.C.P. & S. Edin.

Rev. R. V. TAYLOR. B.A. F.R.H.S.

THOMAS WILMOT. L.R.C.P. Lond. M.R.C.S. Eng.

BUTLER WOOD.

PREFACE.

—◦⟩ω⟨◦—

THERE is poetry everywhere; in the green fields where the flowers watch the rising and setting of the sun, and where the blush of beauty and the breath of song are married in a communion of the spiritual; in the blue sky with its benedictions of sunlight, starlight and moonlight, folding us, as it were, in its soft dewy arms and whispering the serenity of heaven; in the streets of the crowded city, where wealth and poverty, luxury and rags, vice and virtue, hold uninterrupted carnival. No less true is it that the love of poetry is as universal as poetry itself. It is the talismanic key that unlocks the door of every heart. It is the soul's vision of delight; the bud and flower of its primal bloom.

It is the poet's high privilege to sit above the world. Within his heart burns a fire which is quenchless, and his utterances never die. Through all time his song has floated over the world like the voice of an angelic choir chanting their hosannahs in the far-off empyrean. The poet is the herald of the coming time. He stands in the van of progress pointing the onward march of the ages. Though he be clad in "hodden gray" like Scotia's gifted bard his sway is more than regal.

The aim of the editor of this work has been to bring together the best poems, with original biographies of their authors, who were by birth or residence connected with the Parliamentary Division of the Spen Valley. It may be that readers of the volume could be found who would hardly designate some of the contributions by the name of 'poetry.' The authors of these have evidently been inspired with the poetic afflatus in a minor degree. Some of the poems rise to the highest humour and humanity—brilliant similes and homeliest metaphors abound. Others are full of dash, and strength, and sweetness. They alone compel to admiration, by reason of the hardihood of the intellect that created them. Some approach as nearly as possible to mediocrity as they can safely descend, which makes one wish they had kept to prose or refrained from versifying altogether.

However that is a question that is not desirable to dive into too deeply. As a local work it cannot fail to be interesting, and that interest has been evinced in its appearance is amply proved by a glance at the list of subscribers—the majority of whom reside in the district peculiar to the authors dealt with.

By far the greatest interest has been centred in Herbert Knowles — the talented Gomersal poet—many of the subscribers having ordered copies of the book simply to have something in volume form to perpetuate his much-beloved memory. Alderman Woodhead, J.P., of

ALDERMAN JOSEPH WOODHEAD, M.P.

Longdenholme, the Member of Parliament for the Spen Valley, wrote as follows :—

HOUSE OF COMMONS, LONDON,
Dear Sir   May 27th, 1892.
I enclose order for ten copies of your "Poets of the Spen Valley," and trust it may prove a success in every way, as a contribution to our local literary history. If you had no other name than that of Herbert Knowles, that alone to every lover of true poetry would be sufficient to make the book attractive.
                With best wishes,
                    I am dear sir,
                        Faithfully yours,
    DR. FORSHAW.   JOSEPH WOODHEAD.

This high tribute to the genius of Knowles, from a gentleman of such literary eminence as Alderman Woodhead, is specially valuable, and in the procuration of subscribers has been very helpful.

The Editor desires to acknowledge the great indebtedness he is under to the gentlemen who have so generously contributed the original biographies of the different poets; and he would take this opportunity of pointing out that they alone are responsible for the accuracy of the statements that appear in the memoirs. He would also heartily thank the following gentlemen for innumerable kindnesses and for assistance given during the progress of the work :—Alderman Woodhead, M.P., Dr. J. A. Erskine-Stuart, F.S.A., Mr. John Oddy, Mr. J. H. Knowles, Mr. John Firth, Mr. Frank Peel, Mr. Butler Wood, Mr. Chas. A. Federer, L.C.P., Mr. W. Venables Rhodes, and Mr. E. Mortimer.

In conclusion, the Editor would state that the Rev. Patrick Brontë, who resided at Liversedge, and was vicar of Hartshead-cum-Clifton, was dealt with in his volume entitled "The Poets of Keighley, Bingley and District," published last year. He points this out, feeling sure that many of his readers would expect to find some account of the reverend gentleman in the forthcoming pages.

WINDER HOUSE, BRADFORD,
June 21st, 1892.

CONTENTS.

Contents.

Contents.

List of Subscribers.

His Grace the Right Hon. and Most Rev. E. W. BENSON, D.D. D.C.L. Lord Archbishop of Canterbury.

The Right Hon. the MARQUIS OF LORNE, K.T., LL.D.

Abbey, John..   Bishop Auckland (10)
Ackroyd, George, J.P. .. Bradford (8)
Ackroyd, W., J.P. .. Birkenshaw (2)
Alderson. John .. ..Cleckheaton
Allott. Joseph .. Gomersal
Anderton. W., Esq., J.P. Cleckheaton (2)
Anderton, C. P. .. Cleckheaton (2)
Andrews, W., F.R.H.S. .. Hull
Armitage, Joseph .. Cleckheaton
Armitage, Wm., Junr. ..Cleckheaton

Balderson. Henry .. ..Cleckheaton
Barraclough. David .. Cleckheaton
Bedford, J. P. .. Cleckheaton
Bell, J. H., Esq. .. .. Darlington
Bell. J. H.. M.D. .. Heckmondwike
Bennett, Wm. .. ..Cleckheaton
Benson, Arthur White. M.A. Windsor
Bergh, Miss A. J. .. London
Birkby, Miss Ethel ..Liversedge (3)
Birkett. Francis .. Cleckheaton
Binns, J. Arthur .. Bradford
Blakey, J. Wesley .. Millbridge
Boon, Wm. .. .. New Barnet (2)
Booth, Frank .. Cleckheaton
Booth, George .. ,,
Bottomley, Thomas .. Cleckheaton
Bratherton. Miss .. Bradford
Brearley, Allen .. ..Cleckheaton
Brearley, F. H. .. .. ,,
Briggs, Arthur. J.P. .. Bradford (2)
Briggs. C. H.. Esq. .. Wyke (2)

Briggs, Miss F... .. .. Wyke (6)
Briggs, Miss E. M. .. .. Wyke
Bromley, Miss .. ..Cleckheaton
Brook, Frank .. Cleckheaton
Brook, Alfred .. .. Hightown
Broughton. B., M.A. Heckmondwike
Brucey, Josiah .. .. Liversedge
Burnley. J. .. .. Heckmondwike
Butterfield, Rushworth .. Cleckheaton
Butterfield, Thomas .. Cleckheaton

Carver, George .. Cleckheaton
Chadwick. S. J. .. .. Dewsbury
Clayton, Mrs. .. .. Lightcliffe
Clayton, Mrs. .. Cleckheaton
Clayton, Wm. .. .. .. ,,
Clough, Benjamin .. Cleckheaton
Clough. W. H. .. .. .. ,,
Craven. Joseph, M.P... ..Thornton
Cutts, J. N. D.D.S. .. Morecambe

Daniel, H. C. .. ..Cambridge (3)
Davies, Rev. W. J. .. Cleckheaton
Dickenson. F. .. Birstall

Ellis, J. F. .. .. Cleckheaton
Ellis, Jonas .. .. ..Cleckheaton
Ellison, George, .. Birkenshaw (2)
Ellison, A.E. .. .. Bradford
Emsley, John .. .. Bradford
Emmet, J., Esq.. F.L.S. Boston Spa(3)

Farr, J. B., Esq.   ..   Bradford (5)
Farrow, Dr. ..   ..   ..Cleckheaton
Farrow, Rev. Charles, M.A.   ..   Tong
Fearnley, Sarah ..   ..   Gomersal
Federer, Chas. A., Esq., L.C.P. Bradford
Firth, Col., Sir C. H.   ..   Ilkley (5)
Firth, John   ..   Cleckheaton
Forshaw, W. A.   ..   Bradford
Fowler, Rev. W., M.A.   ..   Liversedge
France, Hiram..   ..   ..Keighley
Frere, Hanbury, M.D.   ..Bradford (5)

Gabb, Rev. J., B.A.   ..   Welburn (3)
Galloway, F. C.   ..   Bowness (2)
Garside, Miss H.   ..   .. Birkenshaw
Garside, Walter   ..   Harrogate
Gaunt, J., B.A.   Dewsbury
Greaves, C. H.   Gomersal

Haigh, Miss E. J.   ..   .. Longwood
Hainsworth, Lewis   ..   Bradford
Haley, Jonas   ..   Cleckheaton
Halliwell, Mrs.   ..   Queensborough
Halliwell, W.   ..   .. Cleckheaton
Hammond, Councillor A. V. Bradford (5)
Hammond, Stocks, B.A.   Bradford (10)
Hammond, Alderman   ..   Bradford
Hartley, George   ..   Cleckheaton
Hartley, John   ..   ,,
Hatton, W.H., F.R.H.S.   ..   Bradford
Heald, Rev. C. W. ..   I. of W. (3)
Healey, John   ,,
Hey, J. G.   ..   Cleckheaton (2)
Hillard, J. W.   ..   ..Cleckheaton
Hind, Abraham   ..   Wyke
Hind, Mrs. F.   ..   ..   ..   ,,
Hirst, F.   ..   ..   ..   London
Holdroyd, Alfred   ..   Cleckheaton
Holdroyd, Joseph   ..   .. Low Moor
Holdsworth, Joseph   ..   Cleckheaton
Howarth, W. H.   ..
Hooson, Jas.   ..   ..   .. Scholes
Hunter, John   ..   Gomersal

Jackson, Herbert   ..   Cleckheaton

Karn, F. J., Mus. Doc.   ..   London (10)
Kaye, W. J., M.A.   ..   Ilkley
Kemp, Rev. Canon, M.A.   Birstall (2)
Kershaw, George   ..   Cleckheaton
Kershaw, Walker   ..   ,,
Kershaw, H. W   ..   ..   ..
King, Rev. Thomas, M.A... Hartshead

Knowles, George   ..   Hightown
Knowles, J. H.   ..   Cleckheaton(9)
Knowles, Dan   ..   ,,
Knowles, F. M...   ..   ..Bradford

Lacy, Benjamin ..   ..   Cleckheaton
Law, Alfred   ..   Cleckheaton (2)
Law, Henry   ..
Longbottom, John   ..   ..Birstall
Livingstone, Alderman   ..   Stanhope
Lewis, J.H., D.C.L.   ..   London (5)

Marley, Rev. Robert, L.Th.   ..   Scholes
Marshall, Mr J., Editor *Northern Echo*
        [Darlington
Mayou, Rev. B., M.A.   ..   Bradford
McCullagh, T. A., M.D., J.P., L.R.C.P.
        [Bishop Auckland
Mitchell, Sir Henry   ..   Bradford
Moody, J.   ..   Cleckheaton
Moorhouse, Benj.   ..   ,,
Mortimer Edward   ..   Bishop Auckland
Mundy, James   ..   Bradford

Navey, Walter   ..   Cleckheaton
Naylor, Thomas   ..   ,,
Naylor, William   ..   ,,
Niven, G. H.   ..   Cleckheaton
Nelson Ralph, J.P.   ..   —
Nornabell, John   ..   Cleckheaton
North, J. S.   ..   Cleckheaton (3)
Nutter, Squire   ..   Cleckheaton

Oates Charlotte..   ..   ..Wyke (6)
Oddy, Chas.   ..   Port Elizabeth, S.A.
Oddy, John, V.S.   ..   Cleckheaton (4)
Oddy, Joseph   ..   Liversedge (2)
Oldroyd, G. H.   Gomersal

Parkinson, Mrs F...   ..   .. Wyke
Parkinson, J. W.   Huddersfield (2)
Paulton, J. M., Esq., M.P., Bishop
        [Auckland
Peel, H. H.   ..   ..   Liversedge
Peel, C. A.   ..   ..   South Africa
Peel, Annie   ..   ..   South Africa
Peel, Edith M.   ..   Heckmondwike
Peel, Frank, Esq.   Heckmondwike (2)
Peel, William   ..   ..   Cleckheaton
Pinder, James   ..   ..   Cleckheaton
Porritt, Arthur   ..   . Birstall
Porritt, Saul..   ..   ..Cleckheaton
Priestley, Mrs.   ..   Gomersal
Proud, John, Esq.   ..   Bishop Auckland

List of Subscribers—*continued.*

+-+-+-+

Rabagliati, A. M.A. .. Bradford
Ramage, A., M.D. .. Seaton-Delaval
Rawnsley, Joseph .. Frizinghall
Reeve, Saml... .. ..Cleckheaton
Rhodes. W. Venables Cleckheaton (3)
Rix, Rev. A. H. LL.D. .. Bradford
Rhodes, Joseph .. Cleckheaton
Rhodes, Josiah. Esq. Heckmondwike(3)
Roberts, Chas. H. .. Gomersal (2)
Roberts, John .. Staincliffe (2)
Roberts. Samuel D. .. Gomersal (2)
Robinson, Benjamin .. Cleckheaton
Robinson, John ..
Ross, Fredk. F.R.H.S .. London

Savory, William .. Cleckheaton
Scholes, Councillor .. Morley
Scriven, Richard Cleckheaton
Scruton, Wm. Bradford
Sellers. Leonard .. ..Cleckheaton
Sibbald, Thos., Esq.. Bishop Auckland
Smith. Arthur ..Cleckheaton
Smith. E. .. Gomersal

Smith. William, Esq. .. Morley
Spivey. Arthur .. ..Cleckheaton
Stansfield, F... .. ..Cleckheaton
Stead, Scholfield .. Cleckheaton
Stead. John James Heckmondwike
Stott. Frank .. Cleckheaton
Stuart, J. A. E.. L.R.C.P. Heckm'dwike
Sturman, E. A. LL.D. .. London
Swires, Robert .. Cleckheaton
Sugden, Fred.. .. Hartshead Moor
Sykes, Rev. F., B.A. .. Butley
Sykes, G. .. ..Cleckheaton
Sykes, John. Esq. M.D. Cleckheaton

Tattersall, W. A. .. Cleckheaton
Taylor. Mrs. T. B. .. Bradford
Taylor, Miss .. Wyke (2)
Taylor, Miss A. W. .. Wyke
Taylor, Miss E. N. .. Wyke (2)
Taylor. Miss J. .. Wyke (2)
Taylor. Rev. R. F., M.A. .. Gomersal
Taylor, Rev. R. V., B.A. .. Melbecks
Taylor, Mr. J. .. Wyke (2)
Taylor, Mrs. J. .. .. Wyke
Tetlow, George .. Cleckheaton
Thompson, R., Esq... Bishop Auckland
Todd, J.. Esq. .. .. Birmingham
Todd, W. .. Heckmondwike

Umpleby, Israel .. Hartshead Moor

Waddington, W. .. Cleckheaton
Whalley, Jonas .. Cleckheaton
Wharton, John .. ,,
Wharton, J. P. .. .. Gomersal
Whitley, J. (for Free Library) Halifax
Wigglesworth, Herbert .. Gomersal
Willingale. T. W. .. Dalton
Wilson, Benjamin .. Cleckheaton
Wilson. Henry .. ..Cleckheaton
Wood, Butler (Free Library) Bradford (12)
Wood. Fred .. Cleckheaton
Woodcock, Bowling .. Cleckheaton
Woodcock. Christopher .. ,,
Woodcock, Samson.. .. Scholes
Woodhead, J. M.P. .. Huddersfield (10)
Woodhouse, John .. ..Cleckheaton
Wood. Ralph .. .. ..Cleckheaton
Wood. John .. .. ..Cleckheaton
Wright, Frank .. Hunsworth
Wright, Wm. .. .. Roberttown

Yates, Mrs. H. .. Cleckheaton
Yates, W. W. F.J.I. .. Dewsbury

JOHN ABBEY.

JOHN ABBEY.

By CHAS. F. FORSHAW, LL.D.

Mr. John Abbey, a true poet of nature, was born in Bradford about 1845 or 1846. In infancy he went to reside at Huddersfield, where he received his education—first at St. Paul's National School, then Senior's Academy, and lastly at Outcoat British. At the age of thirteen his mother died, and John was apprenticed, in 1860, to a jobbing printer at Heywood, in Lancashire, and it was as an indentured apprentice that he first invoked the Muse in a memorial piece to a school superintendent, the poetical reminiscences of whom were printed and circulated through the Wesleyan society. The vicissitudes of trade set Abbey prematurely free from his apprenticeship, and he then joined the office of a Glossop paper, where he found more congenial work in assisting with reports. The opportunity afforded by a journal where the standard of merit was not fixed inordinately high, encouraged Abbey to write poetry, and week after week he had a place in the "poet's corner." After that he seems to have rambled about the country, working as a compositor at Ashton, Stockport, Manchester, Liverpool, Leeds, Dewsbury, Cleckheaton, &c., in several of which places he was called upon to exercise the gifts he possessed for the literary work of a newspaper. In 1867 he called casually at Cleckheaton, and was engaged to help on the publication of the first issues of the *Cleckheaton Guardian*. Here he remained for several years, during which time the paper made progress that necessitated two or three removals to larger premises, new machinery, &c. In this connection it may be averred that for a year or so he was the sole printer and reporter on the paper, and many a time has set up the whole of the paper and provided most of the reported matter which appeared therein. It is also noteworthy that he set up scores of columns without a line of MS. or printed copy before him. Of course, no single-handed journalist could repeat the feat to-day, the paper being at least three or four times its original size. Abbey remained on the *Guardian* about ten years, and it is to his endeavours, to a great extent, that the success of the paper can be attributed; his well-known face was to be seen at every gathering, and he is still held in grateful

B

remembrance by the inhabitants of the Spen Valley district. Leaving Cleckheaton, he joined the Belfast press, but shortly after he accepted an engagement on the *Cleckheaton Advertiser*, where he remained for a short time only, subsequently joining the press at Wigan and Oldham. At the latter place he experienced the great sorrow of his life in the death of his two eldest sons from epidemic. After this, he broke up his home, and we next hear of him at West Hartlepool, where again his services were in general requisition as reader, reporter, sub-editor, &c., the circumstances of the case calling also for the exercise of the editorial faculty, and for some time he wrote most of the "leaders," of which several of the proprietors spoke in complimentary terms. The paper ultimately came to grief, and in 1880 Abbey was invited to join the staff of the *Northern Echo* morning paper as a reporter for a wide district of which Bishop Auckland is head quarters; and to-day his is probably one of the best known figures in South Durham, where he enjoys the confidence of his employers, and is held in regard by the thousands who know him so well. It is his boast that he has worked on morning, evening, weekly, and bi-weekly papers, published at all sorts of prices, and that he has done everything that pertains to a printing office—from sweeping the floors, sorting "pie," lighting the fires, &c., to reporting, sub-editing, and editing. Several of his articles have been reprinted for special circulation, and his collection includes several hundred leaders on all sorts of topics. Abbey married the daughter of a Littletown (Liversedge) man and has five children living. Throughout life he has adhered to the principles of temperance, and has won many prizes in poetical and other literary or intellectual competitions. He is a good musician, but plays by ear, and has often given his services at entertainments, &c. His chief athletic diversion is bathing, in which he is something of an expert. He is a man of robust health and physique, and has always enjoyed excellent health.

England.

—

BRAVELY thou stand'st, supreme of nations thee:
Thy flag of Freedom floats o'er every sea:
Thy hardy sons—with hearts undaunted they
Scorn craven fear when Honour points the way.

The exile's home, of all the lands the best ;
Thy bulwarks, Justice ; Liberty thy crest ;
Thy 'scutcheon pure, bright Honour on thy shield :
Queen of the waves : victorious on the field !

Fairest of all, thy sons' exhaustless theme,
The despot's envy, and the poet's dream ;
On burnish'd page emblazon'd is the name
Of glorious England on the scroll of fame.

A race heroic—champion thou of right,
With peerless lustre, gain'd in many a fight ;
Thy gallant arms, e'er foremost in the fray,
The bay and laurel mark thy onward way.

Proudly thy pennons wave on ocean's strand.
The noble ensigns of a patriot land ;
Thy Union Jack rides on the seething foam,
In faithful vigil over hearth and home.

Thy gleaming sabres, drawn in righteous cause,
Have taught stern lessons to thy haughty foes ;
Thy eagle glance can make the tyrant quail,
And change to hope the slave's and captive's wail.

Duty thy watchword, great is thy renown ;
Thy brow majestic wreath'd with victor's crown ;
The foreign hordes mark well thy steady lance,
Nor dare one step upon thy shores advance.

Grim sentinels, thy frowning towers have stood,
Like sea-kings, lav'd by restless ocean's flood :
Bold in thy strength, thou canst defiance cast,
And check ambition with thy fiery blast !

O'er the whole world thy warrior sons prevail ;
Thy fearless spirit breathes in every gale ;
Britannia's flag. as aye in days of yore,
Scorns the proud foe that would invade her shore.

Land of sweet song, enrich'd by genius' fires,
That tells of triumphs won by ancient sires,
Thy glory burns refulgent in the West,
Proclaiming thee, of all, the brightest, best !

Lines on the Suicide by a Young Woman at Hardsoil Farm.

WHITHER away, lone wand'rer of the night?
What on thy soul hath cast its withering blight?
Would'st thou thus early consummate thy doom,
And brave the terrors of the hideous tomb?

Alas, for thee, thou striken child of woe!
Despair hath dealt thy heart a cruel blow.
For thee no terrors hath the sombre night,
As on to death thou tak'st delirious flight.

Ah! who may tell the horrors of that night,
When reason fled, and heav'n was hid from sight!
When rayless gloom encompass'd thy poor soul,
And unto frenzy victim thou didst fall!

On, on, to death, thy throbbing heart thy knell!
Thy woe, too deep for tears, no tongue may tell.
No friendly hand is stretch'd forth thee to save!
Death is thy heav'n; thy solace is the grave.

Who shall essay thy depths of woe to pierce,
As swift through lonely meadow, sad, yet fierce,
With mien distraught, and fitful, short'ning breath
Thou hurriest on to leap the abyss of death?

The taunts of birth, the cruel gibes and sneers,
Thou didst but answer with thy welling tears
Nor courage hadst thou to return the blows
Which robb'd thy bleeding heart of its repose.

Inspir'd with boldness far beyond thy years,
Thou putt'st to flight thy frailer sex's fears;
Nor carest thou for evening's solemn gloom:
The Mecca of thine hopes is in the tomb!

Now hast thou gained the very gate of death,
With wounded heart, with sighs, and quiv'ring breath!
A groan, despairing wail, a shriek of dread,
And thou hast cast thy lot among the dead!

Who on thy deed shall dare in judgment sit,
And back hypocrisy with Holy Writ?
Who shall presume 'twixt thee and Him to come?—
Shall say thy portion is eternal gloom?

Moonlight on the Hills.

Ye lofty hills, ye tow'ring mountains high,
Whose soaring heads seem lifted to the sky;
With wonder and with awe I view your forms,
Ye giant heroes of a thousand storms!

The majesty of silence reigns around;
All's wrapp'd in stillness deep and most profound;
Naught but the insect's fitful hum is heard,
Or the distant cry of some startled bird.

Could hills but speak—their history unfold—
What scenes they might reveal of times of old,—
Scenes that were noble, righteous, just, and good—
Scenes of wild violence and dark deeds of blood.

Here, in dark ages of. religious strife,
The hunted Christian fled to save his life;
When darkest error fill'd the world with blood;
When martyrs, for the faith, the stake withstood.

Imagination's fired! Fancy's flights are free!
Thoughts fly far back deep into Time's great sea!
The present fades and disappears from sight;
Scenes, strange and varied, pass in rapid flight.

Anon the wind, with fitful, sullen roar,
Comes sweeping o'er the bleak and sterile moor;
The lurid lightning's meteoric flash
Is answer'd by the thunder's deafening crash.

Hark, how the war-note peals along the dell!
Dread harbinger of blood, and work most fell;
Its piercing pibroch sounds the awful knell
Of those who ne'er of victory shall tell.

See the huge ranks of mail'd and martial men,
Whose heavy tread awakes the slumbering glen;
Who, e'er to-morrow's sun shall gild the clouds,
Will sleep the sleep of death in gory shrouds.

And now the foe with thund'ring tread advance—
A thousand arms reflect the sun's bright glance—
They meet!—sword crosses sword with angry clash—
Opposing forces meet with deadly crash!

*   *   *   *

The past is gone; my dreamy vision's o'er;
The moon shines on serenely as before;
A death-like stillness reigns o'er moss and fell,
O'er lofty mountain and secluded dell.

A Sister's Love.

THE love of a sister—how tender and pure,
    When shadow'd by trial's dark cloud;
A love that can nobly all troubles endure,
    When by His chast'ning hand we are bow'd.
When restlessly tossing in languishing pain,
    And fever is scorching our brows,
She'll patiently tend us, nor ever complain
    Of the trouble she on us bestows.
Then cherish thy sister, nor e'er in thy breast
    Let a brother's affection grow cold;
And ne'er let her spirit by thee be distress'd,
    Till He to His arms doth her fold.

When misfortune bears hard on our pathway through life,
    Obscuring the bright star of hope;
When o'erwhelm'd in the vortex of hard-struggling strife,
    And Despair her grim portals would ope;
When toss'd like a wreck on adversity's sea,
    And help would ne'er seem to be near;—
'Tis then we arouse in her true sympathy,
    And our hearts to her's we endear.
            Then cherish, etc.

The love of a sister—'tis matchlessly pure,
    As it flows from her warm, gushing heart;
What balm to the spirit, when comforts grow fewer,
    And friends from our side do depart.
When th' world to our woes is indifferent and cold,
    And to poverty turns a deaf ear—
'Tis the love of a sister, that ne'er waxes cold,
    That in the dark hour can cheer.
            Then cherish, etc.

Ǒħe Ḟirst Ǒransgressiǒn.

WHEN Adam first in Paradise was placed,
His eye the Almighty hand in all things traced ;
On every object saw his Maker's seal—
His soul a mystic awe began to feel.

He saw himself with God-like beauty graced,
As through the bow'rs of Paradise he paced :
He saw all nature vassal to his will—
A splendid triumph of his Maker's skill.

A little lower than the angels he—
Lord of creation—earth, and air, and sea ;
All things combin'd to make his bliss complete;
With all essentials was the world replete.

How doubly happy he !—but no ; for there,
Placed in the centre of this garden fair,
Did grow a tree, with luscious fruit weigh'd down—
The Tree of Knowledge, call'd by God His own.

As debauchee burns with unchaste desire ;
As sparks, when fann'd, develop into fire ;
So this new joy, array'd before his sight,
Doth wean his soul from the' Eternal Light.

O, cursed taste !—but see, with stealthy tread,
The Serpent's victim hide his guilty head ;
Far in the forest's deep recess he hides—
And guilt triumphant o'er his conscience rides.

How odious to him was the beaming light—
Too well he knew the action was not right—
Gladly he welcomes the approach of night :
Conceal'd—vain thought—from the Almighty's sight.

"Adam, where art thou ?" was the awful cry
That echoed loudly through the vaulted sky ;
Its piercing tones the spacious heavens fill—
Earth with the thund'ring cry is made to thrill.

*   ☸   ☸   ☸

Disconsolate and sad, he wanders to and fro ;
Gone the sweet hours of peace he once did know ;
All pleasures on his morbid mind do pall,
And racking thoughts disturb his guilty soul.

Thus is it e'er with rebels to our God—
Sure as they sin, so shall they feel the rod ;
Fore'er be banish'd from Jehovah's face,
Until redeem'd by Christ's all-saving grace.

Henry's Soliloquy.*

If must be so—Scribo, thou reasonest well—
Else whence this pleasing hope, this fond desire,
This longing after notoriety ?
Or whence this secret dread and inward horror
Of falling into nought ? Why shrinks my soul
Back on itself, and startles at obscurity ?
'Tis the ambition that stirs within me ;
'Tis ambition itself that points out an hereafter,
And intimates undying fame to my aspiring soul.
Fame ! thou pleasing, flattering thing !
Through what variety of trying circumstances must I pass ;
What calumny and slander must I endure !
And, after all, must bear the dread of base responsibility.
The wide, the unbounded prospect lies before me,
But shadows, clouds, and darkness rest upon it.

Thus have I two alternatives—obscurity and fame.
My bane and antidote are both before me.
This but ranks me with the base herd of nameless mortals,
But this informs me I shall never die.
Myself, secure in my boundless wealth, can smile
At the idle taunts and malicious obloquy of envious foes,
And defy their spleen ;
The town shall pass away, Herbert himself grow cold and
   shy,
And W*ds**th be a foe,
But I shall flourish in immortal wealth,
Unhurt amid the war of ratepayers,
The wreck of editors, and the crash of *boards.*

* "Henry" was the Chairman of the Cleckheaton Local Board, 1867 or 1868.

MISS LUCY ETHEL BIRKBY.

BY THE REV. JOSEPH STRAUSS, M.A. PH.D.

PRINCIPAL MINISTER OF THE BRADFORD SYNAGOGUE, AND
LECTURER IN ORIENTAL LANGUAGES AND LITERATURES AT THE
YORKSHIRE COLLEGE, VICTORIA UNIVERSITY; DEPUTY
EXAMINER IN GERMAN AT THE ROYAL
COLLEGE OF PRECEPTORS, ETC.

———

MISS ETHEL BIRKBY was born at Liversedge on the 30th of September,
1873. She has made many pleasing contributions in prose and verse
to the local papers. Though probably the youngest author in this
volume, for many years past Miss Birkby's contributions have been
looked forward to by the reading public with more eagerness than any
other local author. She has been successful in carrying off first honours
in each of the numerous competitions in which she has taken part.
The titles of some of her prose writings are as follows : " Brother and
Sister," " The Pride of Victory," " The Ghost of the Haunted Bath,"
" In Days of Old," " Within Sound of the Sea," etc., etc. With
regard to her poems she has been equally successful. Her style is easy,
her diction graceful, and her verse flows smoothly. We give a few
specimens, which show her talent in serious as well as humorous poetry.

———

"A Memory."

———

WHEN the field-flow'rs close their petals
And the night-tide gathers round ;
When the birds are flying homeward,
And the shadows strew the ground ;
When the children's play is over,
Hushed their laughter's merry peal ;
Then a host of tender memories
Through the distance softly steal.

With a rush of sudden longing
  Comes a scene before my eyes—
Gleaming, glittering in the sunlight,
  A broad stretch of ocean lies ;
A long line of foam-touched billows
  Break across the yellow sand,
While in sharp and stately outline
  Sea-washed headlands nobly stand.

With a touch of ancient splendour
  Stand the ruined castle walls,
And athwart the shattered gateway
  A broad ray of sunlight falls ;
O'er the rocky coves and inlets
  A deep summer stillness lies ;
From the steep cliff-sides rise echoes
  Wakened by the sea-birds' cries.

Then I see the place by moonlight :
  Music rises on the air,
And those dear, old, terraced gardens
  Come before me broad and fair ;
Midst the crowd are forms and faces
  That I long for now in vain ;
Ah ! my sea-side friends and comrades
  Shall we ever meet again ?

Crowding one upon the other,
  Just as when I saw them last,
Esplanade, cliffs, bridge, and gardens
  Loom from out the happy past.
Friendly hands are stretched to greet me,
  Well-known voices strike my ear,
And for one brief joyous moment
  I am almost with them there.

" Stay forever, fleeting vision ;
  Stay before my longing eyes ! "
Yet e'en as the words are uttered
  The fair picture fades and dies :
Those bright scenes all swiftly vanish
  Like a leaf upon a stream,
And my outstretched hands grasp nothing
  But a memory and a dream.

Nobody Knows.

WHEN Miss Elsie goes walking in search of wild flowers,
And comes back without them in two or three hours ;
Did she find something better ? each face clearly shows
The reply to this question is " Nobody knows."

When young Hudson calls on us and gives himself airs,
And drops half the teacups and falls over chairs ;
No one knows when he tells us he's just come from Rome,
How we wish he had stopped there and never come home.

When dishes are broken, the cook blames the cat—
Now who in creation could contradict that ?
And when cats meet policemen down area stairs,
No one knows that's a game in which two may go shares.

When Dick scans his visage with stern looks and grave,
And gets the impression he's needing a shave ;
How they'll find out the spot where his moustachio grows,
Without a strong microscope, nobody knows.

When sour apples and gooseberries no more are seen,
And Master Ted's rosy face looks rather green ;
A connection of facts might wonders disclose,
But no one connects them, so nobody knows.

When little Jack hides 'neath the broad window seat,
Just to see " the nice gentleman that brings sister sweets";
No one knows when she finds him why sister turns red
And tells nurse quite crossly "take that child to bed."

There are some who search for the tune of the breeze,
And others who can't " see the wood for the trees ";
But out of quite half the events that befall,
What we say we know least of, we know most of all.

A Rule for Life.

READING my inmost heart, what do I see ?
The actions of to-day engraven there ;
A memory that goes with me everywhere ;
And dreams of future days—these are the three.

And which of these, oh! sages, can ye tell,
　　Shall hold the foremost place within my heart,
　　And so usurp the whole, yielding no part
To those two others that do inly dwell?

A hollow voice rolls down the ranks of Time,
　　"Cherish the first thy memories of the Past;
　　Gather those records grey and hold them fast;
So thy life's bells shall ring their sweetest chime."

A new voice breaks upon my listening ear—
　　"The Past is gone," it says, "so let it go;
　　And of the future who may say or know?
Cling to the Present then and have no fear."

"Not so," the Future cries; "spend not thy days,
　　In waiting on to-day; stretch forth thy hands
　　To name and fame to come, and lordly lands;
So shalt thou earn from men their highest praise."

The voices die away, but all their words
　　I still hold in my heart and ponder there,
　　Until their hidden meaning, shining fair,
Guides my weak fingers to the sought-for chords.

At last I read aright—this is the key :—
　　Let all the three have place—so shall the Past
　　Lend wisdom to the Present ; and at last
The Future's joy shall dawn eternally.

Two Castles.

Once on a time, in years gone by,
We played together, you and I ;
We built a castle all of sand
Fit for a prince in Fairyland :
And we quite thought that it would last
Until the day was fully past.
The sea flowed onward in its might,
And swept our castle out of sight ;
So when we came to it again
We searched for it, but all in vain ;
Despite of all the work we'd done
Towers, walls, and gardens all were gone.

Once on a time in after years,
Love filled our hearts with hopes and fears ;
And when the sunlight found its rest
Amid the rose-clouds in the west,
We built another castle fair,
A glad frail day-dream in the air;
Hope gilded all its towers with light,
Love reigned in it and made it bright ;
Alas ! I saw that castle fade
Almost as soon as it was made,
For oh ! my darling, you are gone,
And I am here, alone ! alone !

Five Kisses.

HE kissed her first when her baby lips
    Could scarcely his name unfold,
And he led her about with tender care
    Because he was nine years old.

He kissed her again in childhood's time
    When they wandered on hand in hand,
And sailed the boat he called by her name,
    Or told tales of fairyland.

He kissed her once in her girlhood days
    When the summer world was gay ;
And he told his love in the moonshine rays,
    Where the elm-tree's shadows lay.

And he kissed her when,—a woman grown—
    She stood by his side—his wife ;
When she came with her beauty, youth and love,
    To be queen of his heart and life.

He kissed her last with a broken sigh,
    Her lips gave no answering breath,
For her voice was hushed and that loving heart
    Was silent and still in death.

But the kiss he laid on those silent lips,
    Was borne to the world above,
Where it shines a link in the golden chain
    That binds him to his lost love.

The Six Bridges.

Above a mighty river
  Known as the stream of life,
Six bridges raise their arches
  Over the water's strife.

All who float on those waters
  Breasting the breakers wide,
Must pass beneath those bridges
  To rest beyond the tide.

One day a youth and maiden
  Sailed from a flowery slope,
Drifted along the current
  Under the Bridge of Hope.

Fresh blew the fav'ring breezes,
  Dancing each foam-touched wave ;
Heart-whole and fair the maiden,
  Handsome the youth and brave.

Sudden the waves grew bluer,
  Bright were the skies above :
For they were idly gliding,
  Under the Bridge of Love.

He clasped her hand and whispered,
  " Maiden I love you well,
More than any man knoweth,
  More than my tongue can tell."

" Be mine and let me shield you
  From trouble, care and strife,
And let us go together
  Over the Stream of Life."

So on they sailed together,
  Happy without alloy,
And the waters bore them swiftly
  Under the Bridge of Joy.

Here where each laughing ripple
    Light from the sunshine caught,
They would have stayed forever,
    Thinking forever short.

Swiftly the stream grew darker,
    Heavy their hearts with fears ;
For they were tossing wildly
    Under the Bridge of Tears.

Hushed was the girl's gay laughter,
    Saddened her joyous eyes ;
But Hope cried, "after shadow
    Fresh sunshine shall arise."

The waves grew slowly calmer,
    The darkness fled away ;
But their faces bore times' impress,
    Her golden hair was gray.

Their gaze was fixed beyond them,
    No longer dimmed by tears ;
They passed with quiet spirits
    Beneath the Bridge of Years.

The shadows closed around them,
    The waters widened fast :
They now saw closing over,
    The Sixth Bridge—and the last.

But far beyond those arches
    And the dusky shades of night,
They saw the gleam and glitter,
    Of waves of living light.

They did not fear the shadows,
    Nor felt the icy breath,
That swept them o'er the surges
    Beneath the Bridge of Death.

And now their last foe conquered,
    Safe on the other side ;
They only saw the future,
    And passed out with the tide.

Life's sorrows fell from off them
   They both were clothed in white,
In regained youth and beauty
   They sailed through waters bright.

Bathed in eternal sunshine
   The scene before them lay,
Glad voices called them onward
   To those fair realms of day.

Forever and forever
   Where this life's troubles cease,
They rest in endless glory
   Upon the sea of peace.

Quite Another Thing.

"I LOVE a maiden fair to see;"
"Nay, sir, what can that matter to me?
For aught I care you may love a score,
Yes, love them all, and as many more."

"But I love one better than all," said he;
"Then tell your love to her and not to me,
Why linger longer with me to-night?
I can walk alone for the way is light."

"Ah! listen a little longer, Ninette,
Her eyes are blue and her hair like jet;
"I care not to hear, sir, so haste away
And tell your love to her; pray do not stay."

"But then I am telling her now," said he,
"Ah! that is a different matter," quoth she,
"Must I haste away quickly now, Ninette?"
"Just please yourself," said the sweet coquette.

"If I pleased myself I might not please you!"
"It matters not to me, sir, what you do!"
"Sweetheart, don't trifle; I leave you to say
Remain or depart," "Then I think you may stay."

How to Spend Christmas.

How to spend Christmas? there is many a way
    In which to make the swift hours gay and bright,
And cause such happiness that every day
    May be remembered in its onward flight.

In those glad homes where wealth and light abound,
    Listen for laughter's peal and music's flow;
See the fair forms and faces gathered round
    The festive board beneath the lamplight's glow.

The evening passes there in dance and song,
    (Ah, me! how fast time flies when life is fair!)
In mirth and gladness each hour glides along;
    And no one feels the touch of want or care.

But should our days be filled with the sole aim
    Of gratifying pleasure's eager call?
Ah, no! yet be it spoken to our blame,
    Pleasure is often our chief aim and all.

When Christmas comes, it comes for rich and poor,
    Brings for one gladness, for the other grief:
Look at the crowds which daily pass your door
    With none to give them succour and relief.

God counts them as his children, and his love
    Is just as great for them as 'tis for you,
And in the glory of the world above
    There are of this world's beggars not a few.

Bestow on them a smile and not a frown,
    Give them a fraction of your bounteous store;
And know from heaven Christ is looking down
    And will forget your kindness nevermore.

c

Let Christmas make you tender, patient, kind,
    Let each bright day be marked with brighter deeds;
And if you once begin you soon will find
    That one good action to another leads.

Up and be doing then, or you will dream
    Of what you'll do till Christmas-tide is done,
And then how colourless your life will seem
    Without one epoc in the time that's gone.

Be not afraid brave heart! God will descend;
    Unwavering still pursue your joyful way:
And ah! what joy when steadfast to the end
    You live with God a heavenly Christmas day.

A Ball-room Alphabet.

A   was an Angel, B was a Ball,
C   was her Card, D her dances with all,
E   was her Eyes, and F was her Fan,
G   stood for Glances that killed every man.

H   was the partner who said it was Hot,
I   had a vague Idea that it was not,
J   she thought Jolly, and K was (K)onfiding,
L   the Lieutenant was not worth defining.

M   was Mistaken and thought he could dance,
N   wore a blue Necktie his charms to enhance,
O   was an Ogre, and P his Proposal
Q   his Queer word when he got—her refusal.

R   was the Rogue, and S his deep Snares,
T   was their *Tête-a-tête* up on the stairs;
Unequalled Victory followed I guess,
For W was the Whisper in which she said Yes.

Remember or Forget.

They both are young, and love and life seem fair,
　But they must part, for parting comes to all;
And pointing where a bird flies through the air,
　Over the waves, where dying sunshine falls;
He says, "Away out there I soon shall be,
　Lost to your call and sight, but, darling, yet,
Remember sometimes all you are to me?"
　She answers softly, "I shall not forget."

Three years have passed—has he forgotten? No,
　He treads once more, at night, the London street,
But pauses where a carpet o'er the snow
　Is being trod by thin-shod, dainty feet;
He sees *her* face blanch 'neath the carriage lights,
　An old man holds her arm, the door is shut,
He turns away into the dreary night
　And in a strong man's pain cries "She forgot."

Oh! mammon at thy shrine we may not know
　How many hearts and lives are laid in tears,
How many scars, masked by thy diamond's glow,
　Are borne in aching silence through the years.
Did she forget? No, when they meet he hears,
　'Mid ball-room crowds, the tale of fortunes lost,
To save an ancient name from public jeers
　Silence was purchased at her bitter cost.

A moment then her hand lies in his own,
　"I spoilt your life," she says, "forget, forgive,
My own is ruined too, not yours alone,
　For in my heart the past will ever live."
"Forgive you, yes!" he says, "forget you, no!
　Though bitter sweet, old memories last, and yet
Will *you* remember still?" she answered low,
　"Shall *I* remember? would I could forget."

Far, far away upon a battle plain
   The eyes of night shine quietly, softly down,
As though in pity of the human pain
   That lies unaided there upon the ground ;
Towards their light a soldier turns his head,
   "Tell her, oh ! stars, that I did not forget,"
And scarcely is that dying message sped
   Than on his earthly life the sun has set.

A queen of fashion, she, in after years ;
   People envy the lot before her spread,
For no one sees or recks the bitter tears
   In memory of the past so often shed.
Though he to whom her hand and life she sold
   Never may hear one murmur of regret,
Her heart lies buried with that love of old,
   Remembering always, never to forget.

Spring.

———

GAY Spring is come ! How all the earth rejoices !
   No more we feel cold wintry's icy blast ;
The air is filled with sounds of twittering voices
   That tell us gladly Spring is come at last.

Her hands are filled with tender dewy flowers,
   Warm breezes gather wheresoe'er she treads,
She's heralded by sunshine and by showers,
   At her approach the blossoms raise their heads.

She swiftly glides through every dingy alley,
   She brings the roses to each wasted cheek ;
She causes lips to smile and life to rally,
   In frames that hitherto were frail and weak.

Then let us all, whether old, young or weary,
   Learn from Spring's lesson never to give o'er ;
Trying to make sad lives and homes less dreary,
   And our hearts will be Spring for evermore.

Spring.

A MAIDEN stands, one morn in May,
  By the side of a rippling stream ;
And her eyes wander o'er the landscape fair,
  And the fields of verdant green
    That so lately had worn their robes of white ;
    But now are clothed in the sun's golden light.

The birds are twitt'ring on branch and bough,
  Joyously singing their song of praise ;
And in yonder field the lambs are at play,
  All through the glorious bright Spring day.
    While above the lark sings a sweeter song,
    Than ever was given to mortal tongue.

In the hedgerows green, the maybloom is seen,
  With its blossoms of red and white ;
And the violets sweet in some shady nook
  Flourish, though hidden from sight.
    While children, dotted about in bands
    Flower-garlands weave, with their tiny hands.

Then a prayer goes up from the maiden's heart,
  As she views the landscape o'er ;
That her life, as yet in its sweet Spring-tide,
  May be spotless for evermore,
    And that she may to some poor weary one bring,
    A touch of the brightness and sweetness of Spring.

Nearly—but not Quite.

PATRICK went to see his cousin
  Living in our English state ;
And one day this gallant hero
  Tried to jump a five-barred gate ;
" Well, you know," he said " I cleared it,"—
" What old fellow, you are clever,
  None of us have cleared it ever ; "
" Well," he said, " I cleared it nearly,
  Nearly cleared it, but—not quite."

Patrick's heart was quickly smitten
  By a lady fair to see,
And one day he put the question
  "Darling, will you marry me?"
Home returning said, "I've won her—"
  "Why," we said, "you're very clever,
For she said she'd marry never;"
  "Well, you know, I won her nearly,
  Nearly won her, but—not quite."

One fine morning Pat went hunting,
  All went on without a hitch,
Till his horse, becoming restless,
  Landed Patrick in a ditch;
"Oh!" he cried, "my back is broken—"
  "Poor old fellow we are sorry
Fetch a doctor, hurry, hurry;"
  "Stay," he said, "It's broken nearly,
  Nearly broken, but—not quite."

One day we all went out fishing,
  Pat was watching for a bite;
Suddenly he jumped up crying
  In a tone of wild delight—
"Do you know I've caught a salmon—"
  "What! old fellow you are clever,
We shall envy you for ever!"
  "Well you know I caught it nearly,
  Nearly caught it, but—not quite."

Pat got mixed up in a quarrel,
  And it ended in a fight;
Suddenly he dropped down crying
  "Oh! I'm killed, I'm done for quite;"
Oh! our hearts were filled with horror,
We bent down in pitying sorrow—
Up he jumped—"I'm done for nearly,
  Nearly done for, but—not quite.

Remembrance.

ONLY a little curl of silken hair
　That lies within the shelter of my hand,
Catching a gold gleam from the flickering fire
　And yet.its story is not lightly scanned.

Before my eyes gathers a mist of tears—
　Poor little curl its tale is linked with mine ;
It brings back once again those buried years
　On which life's sunlight ever seemed to shine.

I pierce beyond the walls of my quiet room,
　Beyond the city's din, and dust, and glare ;
A lovely, laughing face lights up the gloom,
　A sweet voice comes like music through the air.

Ah me ! my love, the light of other days
　Dwells in your eyes and lingers in your smile ;
Your gentle hands the veil of years upraise
　Revealing all I loved and lost awhile.

Still are you by my side, so sweet, so glad,
　Just as in life you often lingered there ;
Ah ! why should death of all the choice he had,
　Have chosen you, the fairest of the fair.

I feel your soft touch on my weary head,
　I look into your face so near my own ;
A golden glory round your form is shed,
　The veil drops down and I am left alone.

The firelight breaks the shadows on the wall,
　The gold-touched curl shines brightly in my clasp ;
I yearn no more for days beyond recall
　Holding a fairer future in my grasp.

For darling, is it not your voice I hear
　Soothing my sorrow, lessening my pain,
By whispering of the time each day more near
　When we shall meet beyond the skies again ?

Look down, my love, from out the angel land,
　Know that my heart's dark gloom is breaking fast ;
For hope leads on and with her outstretched hand
　Points to the time when we shall meet at last.

Miss EDITH M. BRIGGS, LL.A.

BY THOMAS WILMOT, L.R.C.P. LOND. M.R.C.S. ENG. L.S.A.

HONORARY ASSISTANT PHYSICIAN TO THE BRADFORD
INFIRMARY; VISITING PHYSICIAN TO THE
BRADFORD FEVER HOSPITAL.

TO ETA.

HADST thou, sweet maiden, lived in ancient days,
  Methinks each daughter of Mnemosyne
Would envy thee thy brightly-laurelled bays,
  Which crown thee queen of truth and purity.
High Jove has planted in thy pregnant brain
  The seeds he sows with such a careful hand ;
  The shoots have risen, and the flowerets grand
Wave here and there—making the barren plain
Into a lovely Eden—for his rain
  Has nurtured them, and soon o'er all the land
  The blossoms he so beautifully planned
Will shed their odours, which will long remain.
Sing on, blest Eta, there shall come a day
When all the world is better for thy sway.

EDITOR.

THIS talented authoress—for whom we predict a bright future—was
born at Westfield House, Wyke, on January 22nd, 1867. She is the
fourth daughter of the late Mr. Jonas Briggs [q.v.]. Some two or three
years ago Miss Briggs was successful in passing the examination and
obtaining the Diploma of Literate in Arts, of St. Andrew's University,
taking honours in English, Anglo Saxon, Moral Philosophy, Logic,
Comparitive Philology, etc. This degree, which is distinctly a ladies'
qualification, is equal in status to the more masculine one of M.A.

Last year Miss Briggs under the *nom de plume* of "Eta" (the name of the Greek letter "E") issued to the world a dainty volume of "Poems." This volume was highly praised by the critical press—many of the leading metropolitan and provincial journals according it unstinted praise—and in our opinion the praise was in every respect well merited, for flashing through every poem like a brilliant meteor, is the glow and glamour of divinest melody, warm, weird imagination, and sparkling glimpses that proclaim the authoress is gifted with all the subtile influences of truest poesy. Some critics say that feminine poetry lacks a certain something that everywhere abounds in and denotes the productions of the sterner sex. But had not "Eta" been personally known to us we should unhesitatingly have asserted that her volume of "Poems" were of masculine growth, so pregnant are they with the characteristic sentiments—which so often abound in the man—but which so seldom are found in the woman. The *Graphic* in noticing Miss Briggs' book could evidently not determine the sex of its author. Says the *Graphic* critic:—"In 'Messages from Hell' "there is perhaps more of the author's own, and certainly a frank un- "veiling of *his* opinions . . . it is only fair, to add that the "motives of his or her muse appear to be excellent." The *Bradford Observer* who are usually *down* on the productions of local versifiers, in this instance accorded the following meed of praise to the volume :— "This little volume of Yorkshire homespun is fresh proof that in many "nooks and byways of the broad county live poetic hearts and tuneful "singers, whose existence is so modestly concealed that it is suspected "least of all by those among whom they live. 'Eta's' instrument "may not be very sonorous or many-stringed, but it rings true and "sweet, and her moral insight is keen. One of her poems marks well "the invalidity of the world's judgments as to 'Failure and Success:'—

"'Judge none blest,
God oft writes 'Failure' where *we* write 'Success.'"

"she says, and in another poem she writes with a scathing pity of "millionaires :—

"A stately equipage,—within was one
"Cursed with great wealth, for all his riches were
"But barriers to his peace of mind,—his gold,
"As mountains rose between his soul and life ;
"For he lived
"No higher than his gold mines."

"That last line is excellent. Indeed, many of her lines are remarkable "for their pith and power. But she is best in her shorter lyrics, notably "in 'Only an Irishman' and 'Little Feet,' the latter of which we "quote : -

" O'er the wide world everywhere,
  March the tiny feet,
Through the flowery fields so fair,
  In the busy street.

Some are gladsome, light, and free,
  Knowing nought of care ;
Others walk more wearily,
  Cold, neglected, bare.

But they all wake echoes sweet
  Of the bygone days,
When *we* walked with 'little feet '
  In Life's pleasant ways !

Miss Briggs' book was noticed in the following manner in the *Journal of the British and Foreign Association of London*, of which Miss Briggs is an honorary member :—" This is a small but attractive little volume. " We predict for it the success it so well deserves, and which, we feel " sure, it cannot fail to obtain amongst thoughtful minds and natures, "capable of appreciating the more refined style of poetry. We are "not, we think, more inclined to praise unduly the sentimental or so "called religious poetry of the day, than most, but we cannot resist, "although the volume before us contains a little of both, giving a word "of strong recommendation in favour of its merits.

" If we see no signs of great poetic genius in the lines of 'Eta,' "yet we can discern a deep and tender insight into character, and a "delicate and sensitive appreciation of the works, and words and feel-"ings of others. The lines on ' Noel Paton's ' immortal picture ' Lux "in Tenebris,' are worth a dozen prosaic descriptions in a ' Royal "Academy Catalogue,' and will be read and appreciated by many a "student of his pictures. The tale of 'A Modern Atalanta,' is clever, "and well told. The other poems are somewhat after ' The Frances "Havergal' style, and come in not a bad second. ' Little Feet,' put "us much in mind of Longfellow's ' Weariness,'

  ' Oh, little feet, that such long years
  Must wander on thro' hopes and tears, &c.'

"The poem is pretty, and the rhyme perfect.

"' Only an Irishman,' contains, we confess, to us, the most stirring "and fascinating lines in the book. 'Eta,' has here struck a chord "which re-echoes in every patriotic British soul. We well remember "the electric words in Mr. O'Brien's speech - " I'm only an Irishman,' "and the spontaneous reply then given by England, and by Scotland, "which stands even more true to day, ' If you are only a *true* Irishman, "you are all we wish for, and most adore, and your hopes shall not be "unfulfilled.'

"'Eta' has reason for no small pride in being the creator of her
"little volume; and in concluding our short review, we wish her every
"success, and we feel sure that :—

'She may hope, as no unwelcomed guest
At our warm fireside, when the lamps are lighted ;
To have her place, reserved among the rest,
Nor stand as one unsought, and uninvited.' "

The following also appeared in the Monthly Magazine for February
last, entitled *Versification :*—"Considering the many volumes of medi-
"ocre verse which are constantly flooding the market, it is a pleasure
"to come across a little book—bearing not only the stamp of merit
"but of originality likewise—between the covers of which are contained
"many a sweet rhythmic line and poetic expression. In the volume
"under notice these excellent qualities are discernible, and 'Eta' is to
"be congratulated on her work. In the poem 'Messages from Hell '
"—suggested, so the authoress tells us, by the book 'Letters from
"Hell '—there is much that is highly commendable, in the diction, in
"the correctness of measure and metre, and chiefly in the sentiment.
"We quote from this poem the following :—

As through dark thunder-laden clouds there breaks
A faint, dim streak of light, so, through the shades
Of misery infinite which shroud my soul
There creeps a half-formed hope: 'Eternity
Shall outlast Hell ; one day, far ages hence
Our sin-curst souls shall be unbound, and know
The joy of pardon.'
                    Were this true, then Hell,
With all its woes, were blest with rays from Heaven !
Alas! that glorious hope fades from my soul,
And all is darkness ! Will it e'er return ?

    .   .   .   .   .

And then before my yearning gaze appears
An Image blest, but undefined—of One
Thorn-crowned and crucified. His face is veiled
From my sin-blinded view; but all my soul
Is swallowed up in longings vast as vain,
To see His countenance divine   to hear
His gracious words—to know His heavenly name --
The Son of God who gave Himself for me ! '

"In similar style to 'The Lost Chord,' there is in this little book,
"'The Message of the Organ,' an exceedingly pretty poem. In 'Shell
"Whispers ' we are treated to quite a different vein and form of verse;

" while, of particular interest to the warm-hearted Irish nation, 'Only
" an Irishman ' sings of that much misunderstood people in words well
" worthy of emulation by many persons who, for lack of proper know-
" ledge of the Irish, speak of them in erroneous terms :—

> 'Only an Irishman! Yet will dawn
> A brighter, more prosperous day,
> When conquering Might shall join hands with Right,
> And Justice shall hold her sway—
> When in one fond link of brotherhood
> Old Ireland and England are bound,
> And the bravest hearts and brightest homes
> In fair Erin's land are found!

" In conclusion, we would cordially, on our own behalf, thank 'Eta '
" for the pleasure given us by a perusal of her poems—a pleasure
" which we trust many of our readers will share by obtaining a volume
" for themselves."

From these notices the reader will see that the subject of this
sketch has issued a work, which is not only highly creditable—for such
an opinion were poor praise indeed—but which in extraordinary inten-
sity and determination of purpose, probably outrivals any previous first
attempt by a member of the gentler sex. This is no extravagant
statement founded on imagination or based on a desire to flatter Miss
Briggs, but formed after a careful and rigid scrutiny of the volume of
which she may justly be proud. In the near future we hope that our
authoress will again issue to the world a volume of verse, and we trust
that its title-page will bear the name that appears at the commencement
of this sketch, for it is a great shame that the identity of Miss Briggs
should be hidden—as it is hidden under her *nom de plume* of " Eta."

Lux in Tenebris.

(Suggested by Sir Noel Paton's picture.)

A LONELY vale, where reigns eternal night ;
Where life and joy are absent ; where the gaze
Of mortal eye shrinks from the dismal sights
Which everywhere surround it ; where the step
Of mortal foot must falter, for the soul,

The God-breathed, brave, immortal soul of man,
Trembles on entering this dread vale.   The pride
Attending rank and fame is trampled here,
E'en to the dust.

In wild confusion lie
The cast-off robes of pomp and lowliness.
A kingly crown and sceptre, thrown aside
By some dread scion of earth's royalty,
Whom mortal terror seized ; a helmet, which
Graced once the brows of some bold champion
Of chivalry, now rusted by the touch
Of Time, lie side by side with garments worn—
The earthly garments of the humble, who
Trod the thick maze of Life, unknown beyond
Their narrow circle.

Noisome vapours dank
Rise from the ground : the hollow roaring wind
Rustles the yellow withered leaves which lie
Scattered, as emblems fit of human life,
When Death, the fell Destroyer, lays his hand
Upon it.   In this awful vale he reigns
As king supreme ; and men, in trembling tones,
Speak of it as the Valley of the Shade
Of Death.   Look round, and see on every side
Signs of his power—there, a human skull
Which once, perchance, had lodgment in a head
Wise beyond common wisdom, now decayed,
Forgotten.   There, a mouldering tombstone stands,
Bearing no name to tell whose dust may lie
Beneath.

But look ! there, where yon glimmering light
Marks the confine 'twixt earthly life and death,
Appears a form, a maiden fair, who casts
Backward her longing eyes.   A shuddering fear
Throws o'er her its dread pall ; her waving hair
Floats on the night-breeze ; her worn, falt'ring feet
The footprints scarce can find of One who fought
And conquered Death ; so, stumbling through the gloom,
Slowly she comes—fair, frail, and fearful ; how
May she attempt to traverse this dark vale
Alone ? Ah, how ?

But turn your wondering gaze
To yonder end of the lone valley, where
The shadows melt in perfect, glorious light
Compared with which the dawn and sunset hues
Of earthly skies, with all their varied tints,
Were dimness.

Through the golden glow there steps
A Form of Wondrous Beauty, Grace Divine..
A kingly glory round Him shines; the gems,
The Monarch's vestments, rich and rare, appear
Unworthy to adorn Him; on His brow
No crown, save one of thorns, and in His hand
No royal sceptre, but a staff—for He,
The Shepherd King of His own chosen sheep,
Will guide them through this vale.

Who can describe
The Face beneath the crown? No glowing word
Of poet, no flight of wild imagining,
Could trace, in faintest outline, half the wealth
Of Majesty and Love Divine, which glows
Upon it. E'en the dread and awful gloom
Of Death's dark shade catches a gleam of light
From the all-glorious presence of the Lord
Of Life.

The trembling maiden sees that gleam,
And Him, the Source of it. Her terror flees;
With peaceful trust she lays her hand in His,
And from His radiant countenance there falls
Upon her upturned face a light, some faint
Reflection of the all-resplendent blaze
Of Glory Infinite, which shines in His.
No word He speaks; He *looks*, and in that gaze,
Not only Love, not only Power, she reads,
But Fellow-feeling; for this Mighty One
Trod, long ago, in loneliness and pain,
This Vale of Death. Here He the Conqueror proved
Of Death and Hell: His footprints, left behind,
Mark where He trod the path of Death—alone.
And, as He leads her onward, from her lips
In peaceful murmur fall the words, "Though I

Walk through the Valley of the Shade of Death,
No evil will I fear, for Thou art with me ;
Thy rod and staff they comfort me." And then
The golden gates are reached, and our weak sight
Can pierce no further, for she enters Heaven !

Le Diable.

LE DIABLE, in his brightest garb arrayed,
Came and before me stood. I, trembling, gazed
Upon him. Beautiful indeed he was—
His brow serenely grand, his deep-set eyes
Flashing beneath : *angelic* they appeared
Upon the surface : but below !—ah, me !
What evil lay in those Satanic depths !
What darkness borrowed from the atmosphere
Which he had breathed through unknown ages, till
It seemed his native air !
                            But to my tale—
In dulcet tones he smiling said, " I come
Upon a matter of so great importance
That many nights and days I have idle been,
Leaving my slaves to do my choicest work,
That I might leisure have to think of it.
You have a friend (so-called), a child of mine—
A favourite child, loved from her infancy
With that excess of love, which to the King
Of Hades doth belong. And you would steal
Her from me—bid her find a place of rest
In cantish goodness—in that sluggish peace
Which bends the souls of men to dwarfish size,
Quenches the glory of Ambition's fire,
And makes them drone out their existence here.
And this career of awful, slothful ease
You have marked out for her, my child—my own !
It shall not be ! " (His visage changed, and lo !

I saw and felt the atmosphere of Hell
Burning around me.)   "Her bright, happy soul
Shall not be marred by you !   This is the life
That I have planned for her.   Listen and judge.
In the dark background of her soul I'll place
Pride, stern and haughty Pride, Passion, and Hate ;
And in the foreground, shedding light around,
Glorious Ambition, leading on the mind
To dizzy heights that mortal eyes will faint
To look at !   No small meannesses nor crimes
Of sordid hue shall e'er cast shade on her.
Men shall bow down to her, and envy her :
Shall yearn for one faint smile from her sweet lips !
The topmost crag of fame, the dazzling light
Of glory shed upon it, shall be hers !
Will you your sanction give ?   If not, I swear
By all the powers of the world to come,
You shall repent !   I, with my mighty host
Of arméd devils, will torment your soul,
Until, at length, you give *her* up !

          Now, dare
You, with your feeble might, your tiny strength,
Wage war against the Prince of Darkness, who
Took up the lance, and hurled the glittering spear
'Gainst Michael the Archangel ?   Long we fought,
And only by untoward chance was I
Expelled from Heaven.   My skill and strength I boast
None on the earth, none in the sea, or sky,
None in dark Hades, and but *One* in Heav'n
Can equal.   How then, child of dust, do you
Think to be victor in the deadly strife ?"
He paused.

              A silence, dread and terrible,
Prevailed ; and then, a sudden beam of light
Shone round me, and the power of Love Divine
Encompassed me ; I felt my soul revive,
And with a calmness unassumed, I made
Answer to that dark form which stood in wrath
Gazing upon me :—"O Prince of Demons, I
Fling down the gauntlet at thy feet !   I scorn
Thy mighty army of 'hell-cats' and fiends,

Thy strength is but the strength of evil, which
Ne'er, in the record of ages, won.
Oh, happy King of Demons, great and small,
Go, summon to the war! I am secure
In that great Power of Justice, whose effects
Thou feel'st in Hades, when the eternal woes
Of anguish and remorse press on thy soul—
In that Divine Sublimity of Love
Which e'en prolongs *thy* days for some good end !
To Him who drove thee from thy seat of bliss,
To Him whose Power defends the right and good,
I trust myself, and her whom I count " friend,"
And *never !*—though the heart of Hades shake
With the tremendous conflict, shall she be
One of thy favoured children !

Now depart.
Back to the kingdom " mourning" for its king—
Back to the capture of the runaways—
Back to the darkness of eternal death !
Farewell ! and visit me no more, I pray ! "
Then, with a mighty flutter of his wings,
And with a fiendish laugh, whose echo still
Rings in mine ears, he left me. And I woke,
And knew it was a dream !

A Modern Atalanta.

" Atalanta, an Arcadian maiden, was famed for her beauty and swiftness of
foot. She made it the sole condition of marriage that her suitor should run a race
with her, and, if he outstripped her, she would be his wife. One of her suitors
took three golden apples, and, as he ran, and she began to distance him, he threw
them, one by one, in front of her. She could not resist the temptation, but stayed
thrice to pick them up ; meanwhile he outran her, and won the race, and a wife."

A MAIDEN, fairest 'mong the fair—her face
Shining with queenly beauty, as a star
Of peerless radiance ; in her glorious eyes
A wealth of midnight splendour—from their depths

D

Gleamed forth a mind of rarest intellect ;
Her features Venus-like ; her rich, dark hair,
Touched with the deep red-brown of autumn leaves.
Rippled around her perfect face, as on
The sandy beach ripple the dancing waves.
A modern Atalanta ; fair and proud,
With many suitors thronging round her, but
She scorned them all, and proudly cried, "He whom
I love must gauge his power with mine, and prove
Himself my equal, nay, superior, in
The race of soul with soul—of thought with thought."
So, one by one, they left her side, to mourn
They that had loved.

       The years sped swiftly on ;
Each day more beautiful she seemed to be,
And lovers came and went, but she loved not—
Felt no responsive thrill.

       At length there dawned
Her day of fate.   Across her path came one
Who well might bear the palm for beauty ; he
As some Greek god in classic grandeur stood ;
The glory of the sunshine in his hair,
And in his eyes a changeful radiance—now
As of the blue of summer skies, and now
As some calm pool of limpid azure depth.
Nor in his beauty lay his fullest power,
For perfect face and form but mirrors were
Of brain with genius fired, and soul aglow
With flashes bright of poet and artist dream.
So comprehensive was his mind, it seemed
A storehouse of all precious gifts.   He was
Noble and generous, crystal-souled and true.
His wealth consisted more in what he *was*
Than what he *had ;* but, being what he was
Assured the future *having.*   He was rich
In hopes, which should, one day, be realised !
And all this dower of heart and brain he cast
Down at the maiden's feet.   She looked on him,
And loved him ! fain would she have cried, "I yield!"
But, while the words still trembled on her lips,
Another came to seek her hand—a man

Who counted gold by tens of thousands : he
Had fair, broad lands, an ancient, noble name.
What more ?   A lack of brains, a selfish heart,
A nature mean and vicious, yet, withal,
A certain pleasing manner.   He had drained
E'en to the dregs the cup of sin.   Could he
A fitting rival be to one who was
Pure, beauteous, genius-haunted ?   Could he win
The " race," and prove his mind " superior " to
This " modern Atalanta's ? "   Yea, his gold
Gilded him with its lustre, made him fair.
He cast the " golden balls " before her, and,
True to the Mammon-spirit of the age,
False to the instincts of her inmost soul,
She stooped to gain them, Atalanta-like,
And he, victorious, claimed her as his bride.

     *   *   *   *   *

And then ?   Long years of gilded anguish ; chains,
Heavier because self-forged, each day seemed bound
More tightly round her ; she had sold herself
To one who loved her not, who but admired
Her beauty, fading hour by hour, for lack
Of Love's bright sunlight.   So her life dragged on
Its weary length.
                And he, who *might*, have been
Her sun, he climbed the rugged steep of fame,
And rested on the summit, where he moved
Among the noblest, and his name was held
In reverence ; but, within his soul, there dwelt
An aching, everlasting loneliness !

Messages from Hell.

(Suggested by " Letters from Hell.")

OH, friend of earth-days—friend, whose soul with mine
Was ever bound in one—I send to thee
A word of warning from these awful depths—
These depths of woe unfathomable.   Stay

The burning fever—vice—within thee; turn
Thy steps towards Truth ere yet it be too late—
I would not have thee here! These scorching flames
Of self-created torture cause my soul
To yearn, as one of old, to save my friends
From such dread punishment, and, Dives-like,
I fain would cry to thee, " Beware! Repent!"

     *   *   *   *   *

Death seized my soul, all unprepared. I woke,
In Hell. A host of hideous phantom shapes
Surrounded me, whilst on mine awe-struck ears
Wild moaning voices fell. A murky light—
The only light this land can boast—prevailed,
Succeeded soon by darkness thick, and dense,
And Indescribable.

                    And thus drew on
My first dread night in Hell!

     *   *   *   *   *

                  Oh, awful world
Of grand illusions! Grim, dread fairy land!
We long for stately mansions, sumptuous fare,
Gay pleasures, gorgeous robes; and, ere the wish
Has passed our brain, behold! 'tis realised:
Only in shadows! All is mocking show!
Our princely mansions melt in dust away;
Our festive revels but delusions are;
We wear our splendid robes, and shiver still
In very nakedness; our royal fare
Appeases not one pang of hunger, nor
Of greed. We leave the feast unsatisfied!

     *   *   *   *   *

Onward I wander aimlessly. This Hell
Daily reveals fresh wonders. Suddenly
I see an eager crowd, hanging upon
The words of one who, on the earth, once bore
The title " Honourable;" yet honour was
A thing unknown to him—a statesman he,
Who wronged his country for the brief-lived joy
Of gratified ambition.

Now, in Hell,
He lies and bribes as he was wont to do,
And still his words find hearing from the crowd,
But with this difference vast—they mock at him
Where once they cheered. They scan him through and
    through
With keen, enlightened eyes, and view him now
In his true colours ; yet perforce, poor souls,
They listen still ; it is *their* doom to hear,
And *his* to speak—a bitter farce to all !

           ❀   ❀   ❀   ❀   ❀

A stately minster pile, o'ercrowded with
A multitude of eager listeners. Rare
Phenomenon on earth, but common here !
These poor lost souls are panting, yearning, now,
For words of once despiséd wisdom, but
They ask for bread—receive a stone ! No lack
Of Teachers, but a fatal lack of Truth !

           ❀   ❀   ❀   ❀   ❀

Think not that this vast world of wailing souls
Illiterate is, Ah, no ! Hell swarms and heaves
With earth's most cultured sons. Philosophers,
Historians, scientists, and poets are here—
Reviewers too, and numerous novelists !
Using their intellect to damn their souls,
They purchased wealth and fame—their life the price !

           ❀   ❀   ❀   ❀   ❀

The memories of the Past crowd round me ! some
Adding fresh torture to my burning soul.
Sins of my youth ! Sins half-forgotten, till
This hell-awakened memory scourged me with
A recollection of each wrong—pure lives
Defiled by sins of mine—hearts innocent
Made guilty, and, crushed 'neath that awful load,
Breaking, and in this place of torment I
Have met the sin-stained souls of those who once
Were bright and pure as angels: now, through me,
This is their awful home. Oh ! sins, sins, sins !
Though through eternal ages I may weep,

I never can atone. For ever must
This biting serpent of remorse inflict
Its cruel sting. Ah, would my soul could be
Shattered! and feel no more its being's pain!

    *   *   *   *   *

Yet I was called on earth—*a gentleman!*

    *   *   *   *   *

Those spectral visions of my sinful Past
Flee for a while. Before mine eyes a sweet
Dim memory floats—the angel-face of one
Whose earthly future I designed to link
With mine! but He, who loved her pearly soul
Too well to have it doomed to such sad fate,
Took her. My darling! would that this sad heart
Might break, and, in that breaking, lose its power
To feel thy loss.

    *   *   *   *   *

                    Another face! of one
Whose life was wreathed with faded hopes and joys,
With long-lost dreams of love. She might have been
A failure, but she proved a grand success:
She lost her life to save it unto Life
Eternal. Now she rests in Paradise.

    *   *   *   *   *

In Paradise! To these hell-weary eyes
A vision fair, yet torturing, hath appeared
Of that blood-purchased home of the redeemed.
Compared with it, earth's loveliest scenes were bare
And desolate! No angel could describe
That beauty infinite. How then shall I?

    *   *   *   *   *

As through dark thunder-laden clouds there breaks
A faint, dim streak of light, so, through the shades
Of misery infinite which shroud my soul
There creeps a half-formed hope: "Eternity
Shall outlast Hell; one day, far ages hence,
Our sin-curst souls shall be unbound, and know
The joy of pardon!"

Were this true, then Hell,
With all its woes, were blest with rays from Heaven!
Alas! that glorious hope fades from my soul,
And all is darkness! Will it e'er return?

     *   *   *   *   *

And then before my yearning gaze appears
An Image blest, but undefined—of One
Thorn-crowned and crucified. His face is veiled
From my sin-blinded view; but all my soul
Is swallowed up in longings vast as vain,
To see His countenance divine—to hear
His gracious words—to know His heavenly name—
The Son of God, who gave Himself for me!

"Such as These."

A STATELY equipage—within was one
Cursed with great wealth, for all his riches were ·
But barriers to his peace of mind—his gold
As mountains rose between his soul and life;
Cursed with the power to choose 'twixt Right and Wrong,
Because he chose the Wrong. Upon his brow
Were wrinkles, born of days of anxious toil
And nights of restless grandeur; for he lived
No higher than his gold-mines.

               As he rolled
Along in empty pride, he chanced to pass
Some humble labourers, from their daily toil
Returning. On his ears their laughter jarred;
A darker frown spread o'er his brow, and from
His lips burst forth an angry growl. "To think
That *such as these* should be allowed to vote
With men of my high rank and influence! But
These Radicals *will* talk and change the times,
Until the grand distinctions 'twixt the rich
And poor shall cease to be.

                    The days are gone
When Might was Right, and these were but as dogs,
To do the bidding of their masters." So
He rambled on.

                         'Tis thus the world has talked
Since first the lion's share of gilded dross,
Or ancient lineage, was accounted stamp
Of true nobility. But, when our earth
Was rife with social discord, there appeared
Upon its scene One, King and Lord Supreme,
Yet, stooping from His heavenly throne, He came
To live and toil with "such as these"—to know
The hardships and the daily sordid cares
Which are their heritage. And so with joy
They heard His Gospel, for He taught that men
One Master have in Heaven. From Him there sprang
The spirit which emancipates the slave
And grants the labouring man his vote. But yet
Abounds that anti-Christ-like spirit which
Denies to "such as these" the right to *live*.
"Exist, work as machines, eat, drink, and die—
Be this your lot!"

                         Methinks the day *will* dawn
When this slow-dying spirt shall be dead,
And God's great world-long training of the race
Shall merge in recognition—full, complete—
Of this grand truth, that men are brothers all!

Mysteries.

A LOVELY child-form, full of promise sweet,
Walking the earth with gladsome, fairy feet,
The rosy hues of dawn scarce passed away
When closed, for ever, was Life's happy day.

Two fair young lives, in Love's sweet compact bound,
Blessed with all precious gifts, and nobly crowned
With well-earned honours—severed, ere the lips
Were cold from sweet first kisses! Dark eclipse!

A fertile brain, devising works of skill
Which, once accomplished, would the nations thrill
With admiration for that genius bright,
When, lo! the spark was quenched in blackest night.

A life, which might have been ablaze with fame
And everlasting glory, sunk in shame,
Fading away in vile dishonour—all
The wealth of talent buried 'neath that pall!

A noble heart, beating for others' good,—
Finding its joy in human brotherhood,—
Stilled in its warmest pulse by Death's cold hand!
Who can these awful mysteries understand?

    *   *   *   *   *

Lo! through the gloom and mists breaks light: when, lost
In dark and trackless wastes of thought, uncrossed
By any soul with Reason's aid, we grasp
A Stronger Hand than ours, in Faith's firm clasp,
And know a Mightier Power than ours still reigns,
A Wiser Love controls our fears and pains.
Then earth's dim mysteries vanish, as a dream,
In view of God, the Mystery All-Supreme!

The Poet's Mission.

TRUTH, from the Eternal heights,
  Calls to mortal men :—
" Who is there with burning thought,
  And with skilful pen?

Hearken ye to these my words,
  Souls of genius rare,
'Tis the mission of the poet
  True things to declare."

Poets there are whose bright, clear thoughts
  Glow with genius-fire,
Uttering soft and pleasing words
  Such as men desire :
Shrining high and gilded vice,
  Flattering lordly sin,
And their songs, so falsely sweet,
  Ready hearers win.
But a shadow, cold and dark,
  Rests upon their fame :
Fair poetic gift is theirs,
  Truth an unknown name !

Other souls there are, whose depths
  Burn with fiercer flame,
Keen as lightning-flash their wit,
  Swift and sure their aim ;
Wrath and malice, bitter scorn,
  Guide their scathing pen,
And fair Truth is hidden thus
  From the view of men.

Such abuse their precious trust :
  But there are who feel
That their mission, high and blest,
  Truth is to reveal.
And, perchance, they thus may lose
  Glory, worldly praise,
Nor around their God-loved names
  Earthly radiance blaze :
But they struggle upward still,
  Truth their living creed—
Theirs the true poetic fame,
  Theirs the highest meed !

Only an Irishman.

Only an Irishman! standing here,
  Pleading his country's cause—
Pleading the common claim of man
  To equal and righteous laws—
Asking that England's far-famed power
  May no curse, but a blessing, be
To subjects in the sister-isle
  Just over the rolling sea.

Only an Irishman! Centuries old
  Is the wound which these words disclose,
For England has striven to make the men
  Of Ireland her bitterest foes.
By the conquerer's power and cruel sword,
  And Oppression's ruthless hand,
For hundreds of years her pride has been
  To crush and coerce the land.

Only an Irishman! Who have been
  'Mong our first in senate and field,
With the brain of power, and heart of fire,
  And courage that would not yield—
Among the chief in the skilful use
  Of the tongue, the sword, and the pen?
Their home was the isle of crime and shame—
  They were "only Irishmen!"

Only an Irishman! Yet will dawn
  A brighter, more prosperous day,
When conquering Might shall join hands with Right,
  And Justice shall hold her sway—
When in one fond link of brotherhood
  Old Ireland and England are bound,
And the bravest hearts and brightest homes
  In fair Erin's land are found!

The Story that Transformed the World.

LONG ago, 'midst Galilean mountains,
  Dwelt a poor despiséd Nazarene ;
Hard He toiled for bread, from dawn till sunset,
  And His life seemed humble, but serene.

Thus He lived, for thirty years, unnoticed,
  Then the sleeping power within Him woke,
And He moved 'mongst men as Teacher, Leader—
  Wise and helpful words of counsel spoke.

Stainless was His life ; but foes were many—
  For the great Reformer's blood they craved.
In their burning fury, to the rulers
  Pictured Him as blasphemous, depraved.

So He died, a Martyr pure and noble—
  Died a cruel death, with courage high,
Teaching all the world the needful lesson,
  How to rightly live, and how to die.

That was all—a sad but brave life-story,
  And a few poor followers left behind.
Search through history's pages, and full many
  Records of like heroes you will find.

Many centuries since have sped their courses—
  Men of wisdom great and god-like power
Have, since then, achieved their life's ambition,
  And enjoyed earth's fame one brief, bright hour.

But throughout the ever-rolling ages,
  This sweet simple tale of Galilee,
Has maintained unequalled, wondrous influence
  O'er the sage, the boor, the bond, the free.

And the Hero of this village story,
  Holds a place beyond e'en poet's dream :
Men of every rank and every nation
  Worship Him as Lord and God Supreme.

He was *only man ?* Then surely never
  Ancient fable, myth, or heathen lore,
Half so wondrous was as this strange picture
  Of a Man whom heaven and earth adore !

The Message of the Organ.

SHE stood in the old Cathedral,
　As the glorious sunset light
Stole in through the storied windows,
　And touched with a radiance bright
All, save the heart of the maiden,
　As in anguish she knelt to pray
For the safety of one who was dear to her,
　In peril, far away.

But the soft, low tones of the organ
　Fell on her weary brain,
As falls on the thirsty flowers
　The gentle summer rain ;
And the heavenly music whispered :—
　"Though awhile ye may parted be,
Ye shall meet again, in the rush of Time,
　Or the hush of Eternity ! "

The music ceased, but she lingered
　Till the twilight shadows grey
Crept slowly, coldly around her,
　Telling of dying day.
Then she rose amid Life's partings,
　To wait for the dawn of Day,
When earth's sorrows and tears shall for ever cease,
　And reunion shall be for aye !

Shadows.

WHY do the shadows come ?
　Why is it not all light ?
Why should the touch of shade
　Fall on this earth so bright ?

Why should the glorious sun,
  Source of the joy of day,
Shedding his light, produce
  Shadows so dim and grey?

Why should the fairest things,
  Brightest, most beauteous, and best,
Ever be haunted by shades
  Which darkly on them rest?

Why should the mind have shades?
  Why should the soul have fears
Cast o'er its brightest hopes?
  And mirth be drown'd in tears?

Why should the purest joys
  Our human hearts can know
Oft have their glories dimmed
  With shadows dark of woe?

List to the answer clear
  That floats upon the air:—
"If earth were cloudless brightness,
  Would it not be *too* fair?"

We cannot bear the splendours
  Of God's unsullied light;
The view would be too glorious
  For our poor human sight.

So our Heavenly Father
  Mingles the light and shade—
Gives to us joy and gladness,
  Causes that joy to fade.

Let us remember the shades
  Fall from His loving Hand
To turn our eyes toward Heaven
  The beauteous sunny land.

And when we reach that city,
  Where the Eternal Day
Reigns in its glorious brightness
  "Shadows" will flee away!

JONAS BRIGGS.

By HERBERT SHACKLETON, M.R.C.S.Eng. L.R.C.P.I.

———

THE obituary columns of the *Bradford Observer* of May 27th, 1891, contained the following announcement :—

BRIGGS.—May 25th, at Westfield House, Wyke, Jonas Briggs, aged 70 years.

Mr. Briggs had for nearly half a century borne a high reputation in the Bradford trade. He was a native of Wyke, where his father, Mr. John Briggs, was a corn miller. He was brought up to the worsted business in the establishment of Messrs. Murgatroyd & Clayton, of Holme Top Mills, a firm which has long become extinct. Above forty years ago he entered into partnership with Mr. George Sugden, also of Wyke, and about 1851 they took Bowling Mills, which had been principally erected for them by the late Sir Henry Ripley, Bart. This partnership has existed until the present time, and the annals of commerce furnish fewer instances of a happier union of interests, or of more uninterrupted success. The business at Bowling Mills embraces the various processes of combing, spinning, and weaving, the fancy trade being made a speciality. The firm employ about a thousand workpeople. In the management of the business Mr. Briggs took a prominent part, and brought to his work all the qualities essential in the management of a large commercial enterprise, not the least important being his methodical habits and the constant personal superintendence which he gave to all the details of his business. As a frequenter of the Exchange he was always to be relied upon for punctuality in attendance, and his probity and uprightness of character made him highly esteemed. Mr. Briggs always shrank from taking any prominent part in public life. The only movements of this character with which he was identified were those which resulted in the erection of the Bradford Exchange and the Victoria Hotel, both schemes enlisting his warmest support and sympathy. In politics he was attached to the Liberal party until 1885, when he joined the ranks of the Unionists.

Mr. Briggs was from his youth connected with the Congregational body, and attended Westfield Chapel, Wyke. To this place of worship he was much attached, and gave with no meagre hand towards its maintenance. Mr. Briggs resided all his life at Wyke, where his death will be regarded as a loss to the community. Many years ago he purchased Westfield House and estate. The deceased gentleman had been in failing health for about a year and a-half. He leaves a widow, three sons, and five daughters. Mr. Briggs had been a lover and writer of poetry from his youth—though he never sent his productions to any magazines or newspapers. The poems quoted are selected from original manuscripts, the composition of the last fifty years.

A Smile.

What is it often cheers the soul,
   When darkness gathers round it ?—
That makes a thrill of pleasure roll
   When deep despair had bound it ?
It is a smile,—the smile of love,
Sweet emblem of the joys above.

What is it soothes the mother's heart,
   When o'er her sickly child she's leaning ?—
That breathes new life through every part,—
   So noiseless, yet so full of meaning ?
It is a smile,—the smile of love,
Sweet emblem of the joys above.

O what can ease the love-sick swain
   When prostrate at her feet he falleth ?
Spell-bound in Cupid's endless chain,
   He loves, he sues, he fondly calleth !
It is a smile,—the smile of love,
Sweet emblem of the joys above.

On Death.

Oft have I thought how shall I meet
   My last great mortal foe ;
Shall I him spurn ? shall I him greet ?
   Will all be joy or woe ?
Oft have I thought the ground I tread
   I soon shall tread no more ;
But strangers tread it in my stead,
   Fresh footprints mark the floor.

And shall I leave no trace behind
   Of love, of joy, of home ?—
No sympathizing friends to bind
   Their heartstrings round my tomb ?

I ask no monumental pile
   To tell where I may lie ;
I court not the historian's smile,
   Nor the poet's lyric eye.

But this I ask—to build a wall
   Of noble deeds of love,
To stand long after I may fall,
   Pointing towards heaven above.

I ask to wipe away the tear
   From the orphan's blanchèd cheek ;
To comfort, strengthen, and to cheer
   The needy, poor, and weak.

I ask to lend a willing hand
   Where virtue lies oppressed,
Where righteousness and justice lie
   Unheeded and unblessed.

I ask affection's ties to bind
   With love's enduring power,—
Bid manly thought and noble mind
   Swerve not in darkest hour.

And this I ask—the beck of God
   To guide me on my way,
To tread the steps His Son hath trod
   Up to eternal day.

God is Love.*

With heaven's high arch above us,
　God's earth beneath our feet,
With friends around who love us,
　Great God, this day we meet.

We meet to sing Thy praises,
　To worship only Thee ;
Now may Thy Spirit raise us
　All glorious things to see !

True faith and holy feeling
　To each, to all bestow ;
Keep earthly thoughts from stealing
　The love to Thee we owe.

May guardian angels hover
　Around us from above,
May every soul discover
　This truth—that " God is Love."

Behold His love in nature,
　His goodness unto all,
He blesses every creature,
　However great or small.

His spirit—love excelleth
　All other love beside,
It is the love that dwelleth
　Whatever may betide.

This love knew no beginning,
　Its end shall never be ;
It found the soul all-sinning,
　It blessed, and set it free !

Its height we cannot measure,
　Its depth we do not know,
Its breadth exceeds earth's treasure,
　Its value—who can show ?

* Composed for the Halifax Sunday School Jubilee.

Morning.

HAVE you seen the sun rise in his glory,
  Kiss the dew as it lay on the grass,
Clear the valley all misty and hoary,
  That the breath of the morning might pass?

Have you heard the sweet songster's first chorus
  Break the stillness of meadow and grove,
When the half-hazy curtain hung o'er us,
  E'er the rumble of day was amove?

Have you seen the sweet flower's glassy beauty,
  When the dew-drop was hung on its lip;
Have you e'er amid life's sterner duty
  Loved the nectar of morning to sip?

Gratitude.

LET grateful aspirations fly
To God, the Source of every joy;
As birds soar upward to the skies,
So may thank-incense ever rise!

As flowers shed fragrance round our home,
May grateful songs around Thy throne.
As run the rivers to the sea
May thankful spirits flow to Thee!

As points the needle to the pole,
So points to Thee the grateful soul;
Let Nature then conspire to raise
A song of gratitude and praise.

The song shall in the valleys rise,
The mountains lift it to the skies,
The seas shall praise Thee in their roar,
And spread the song to every shore.

The angels in high heaven above
Shall chant their sweetest strains of love,
The universal hosts shall bring
Their grateful offerings to our King.

The earth, the air, the sea, the sky,
In noblest strains together vie,
E'en then, the sweetest song shall be
The song of sinners saved by Thee!   .

An Angel's Whisper.

DEEP down in the depths of darkness,
    Where all was black as night,—
Not a rift in the clouds above me,
    I yearned for one ray of light.

Encompassed around by sorrow,
    Not a star of hope in sight,
I prayed to my Heavenly Father
    To send His glorious light.

I waited, I waited, waited,
    Expecting something bright;
An angel whispered in my ear—
    "I come from the land of light."

"I come to guide, to guard thee,
    To be ever at thy side,
Though thy path be rough and stormy,
    I will still with thee abide."

"Fear not all the powers of darkness,
    There is a pure light above,
No earthly sorrow can destroy,
    'Tis the heavenly light of Love."

"Look up, look up, and thou shalt see
    That ever blessèd sight—
The Holy God, the Infinite,
    In His own glorious Light!"

G. W. BENNETT.

By CHAS. F. FORSHAW, LL.D.

Mr. BENNETT was for some years employed as an assistant by Mr. J. C. Scott, Draper, Cleckheaton, and during that time wrote several poems. During his residence in the district he took an active part in the various religious institutions of the town, and was highly respected by a large circle of acquaintances.

The Farewell.

Ah ! I am far away from thee,
　　And from the friends I love so well :
And, while I'm sailing o'er the sea,
　　I softly breathe a long farewell.

'Tis closing eve, and Briton's isle
　　Is gently fading from my view,
Yet, e'er the veil of darkness falls,
　　I'll gently breathe my last adieu !

Before the morning twilight dawns
　　I shall be far from England's shore ;
And, ere I close my eyes in sleep,
　　I wish to look on thee once more.

Oh ! glorious land ! I view thee still :
　　May heaven's sweet smile upon thee shine
And God, the guardian of thy hills,
　　Bring peace and love to thee and thine.

I'll sweetly think and breathe a prayer
　　For thee whom I have left behind ;
And ask for God's protecting care
　　To be thy guard, and also mine.

The tears now streaming down my cheek,
　　Affection sheds them all for thee ;
Yet they are all by far too weak
　　To show how dear thou art to me.

Yet while I'm far away from thee,
　　And from the friends I love so well,
I breathe a message o'er the sea,
　　And that shall be a fond farewell!

And should I never more return
　　But die beyond this dark-blue sea,
Before my lips are closed in death
　　I'll gently breathe a prayer for thee.

To the Ocean.

Roll on, thou mighty Ocean, roll!
　　Dark are the billows of thy azure deep;
Thy music loves the heart of every soul;
　　E'en lulls the sailor-boy in realms of sleep.
I love to linger on thy ocean-shore,
And listen to the billows as they roar:
They seem to breathe a music, though unknown
A melody to which we all prefer;
A sound that dwells upon the lingerer's ear
With a deep thrill, the sweetest ever known.

Oft have I laid upon thy gentle breast,
When calm thy brow and motionless thy crest;
And sported on thy waters bright and clear,
Without the least of accident or fear;
Bright were those hours, when I was wont to be
Borne on thee, brilliant, buoyant, dark-blue Sea.
I've watch'd the little wavelets as they roll'd
Along their course, majestically bold;
And, when the sun was shining out its day,
I've watch'd them sparkle in that silent ray.

What can compare to thee, oh, mighty Deep,
　　Laving thy tide upon each distant strand;
Thy monstrous billows in their wildness sweep
　　Deeds of destruction on our coast-bound land.
Didst thou not know the rock, and once the cave:
Ah! they are lull'd beneath thy ocean wave.
Whole empires have submerged beneath thy tide,
But thou rolls o'er them, Ocean, far and wide.
These are thy deeds; they must remain with thee
Through the vast ages of Eternity!

W. BRINDLEY BOON.

By WALTER J. KAYE, M.A.

PRINCIPAL OF ILKLEY COLLEGE, EDITOR "THE LEADING POETS OF SCOTLAND," "THE HISTORY OF RAWDON SCHOOL," ETC.

THOUGH not a native of the Spen Valley, Mr. Boon resided in Cleck-heaton for twenty years; he therefore comes well within the scope of the work. Mr. Boon who was born at Burslem in 1843 and is now residing in London, attached to the Salvation Army as one of its officers. Says our author in a letter received from him in February, " Ten years have gone since I left Cleckheaton, nevertheless there is always a warm corner in my heart for what is practically my native town." Mr. Boon while in Cleckheaton was a constant contributor to the *Guardian*, and other journals, and though of late he has practically discarded the Muse, he occasionally finds time to ventilate his views in verse.

Links.

WE are not strangers here on earth,
   Alone, and all unblest ;
Nay from the moment of our birth,
   Down to our final rest,
To thoughtful eyes, the closest ties
Link us to all in earth and skies.

An earthen vessel, yet 'tis fill'd
   With light and fire divine,
So God, the mighty one, hath will'd
   To link our souls with time.
We are not strangers—we are one,
With shining glow-worm noonday sun.

The perfumed breath of clover fields,
    The smell of new-mown hay,
The odour that the bluebells yield,
    The hawthorn flowers in May;
These wake from sleep the music deep,
Till richest harmony we reap.

The restless ocean's wildest wave,
    Finds echo in our heart,
We, like the ocean, would be brave,
    And nobly do our part;
The waves are free, yet bounds we see,
Like man's free-will and destiny.

Unmoved, the grand old mountains stand,
    As watch-towers o'er the earth;
Like giant waves held by God's hand,
    And frozen in their birth;
Oh! how we long to be as strong—
No wind, or storm should mar our song.

In crystals, shaped by unseen hand,
    The snowflakes lightly fall,
The strong wind sweeps them o'er the land,
    It grasps and moulds them all;
We too are born like snow and storm,
With power within to change earth's form.

The spring time comes, the Master's hand
    Drives on each atom small,
They bend and whirl at His command,
    In beauty rise and fall,
Not snow-wreaths here, but flowers appear,
Wave crests from seas of beauty near.

A thousand links our memories add
    To each familiar face
To children's words, and laughter glad,
    To every well-known place:
Our words are steeped in memory's power
And gain new meanings with each hour.

HAROLD C. DANIEL.

By WALTER J. KAYE, M.A.

PRINCIPAL OF ILKLEY COLLEGE, YORKSHIRE.

THOUGH not a native of the Spen Valley, Mr. Daniel for some time
resided at Liversedge, and whilst there, was an active contributor to
the local press. He was born at Loughton, in Essex, in 1866. His
father was a wealthy London merchant, who unfortunately lost his all
in that too well-known great failure of Overend & Gurney's Bank, on
Black Friday, 1868. This blow prostrated our author's father with a
serious illness from which he never recovered. Mr. Daniel had
belonged to one of the City Livery Companies—the Salters—and our
future poet therefore entered the City of London Freeman's Orphan's
School when but eight years of age. Here he remained for a period
of seven years. On leaving school he had life's battles to fight the
best way he could, and occupied various positions as clerk, correspondent, and manager. Mr. Daniel, who is at present residing at
Cambridge, is devoted to art and literature, and we forebode for him
in this department a no mean future. Professor J. S. Blackie writes
to him as follows :—" Your subject is good, and your style is good.
" Be faithful to your genius, and never write without a strong inspira-
" tion." Mr. Walter Besant, the eminent novellist, also wrote him :—
" Your poems have merit, and show promise." We may remark that
acting upon the advice he received from Prof. Blackie and Mr. Besant,
Mr. Daniel has been under a course of study which should be highly
beneficial to him. He is now engaged on a long epic, which he hopes
shortly to publish. The poem we quote is from the *Cleckheaton
Guardian.*

Ignatius.
A Tale of the Roman Arena.

BACK floats the memory to indulge,
 In stories of the Roman rule,
Which wandering poets e'er divulge,
 To grast the glitt'ring rod of Fame,
 And plant an everlasting name,
 By some imposing miracle.

The good Aurelius is gone,
  And virtues reign with him has ceas'd ;
Commodus sits upon the throne,
  A potentate of lust and feast.
Oh ! Marcus, gaze upon thy son,
  And view the contrast of thy reign ;
The loving hearts thy virtue won
  Now bleed, and leave a crimson stain.

Once more we see that frowning form,
  Upon that awful throne of state,
The gath'ring of the coming storm,
  The victim calmly face his fate.
The senators around him stand,
  And though in pity some are bent,
They dare not thwart the grim command
  By showing forth their discontent.
There, like a lion strong in pow'r,
  He sits his throne in sullen mood ;
His mighty voice is heard to tow'r,
  And call forth for the victim's blood.

Silence succumbs, and then we see
  A youthful form approach the throne ;
Noble in grace and majesty,
  That e'er fair maid's eyes shone upon.
With hand outstretch'd toward the sky,
  With eyes that pierce with scornful stare,
His attitude seems to defy,
  The danger of the lion's glare.

" Tremble, oh ! King, " he cries aloud,
  " When death in spectral robes appears ;
For when encircled in thy shroud,
  Think not to claim a nation's tears.
A greater King reigns far above,
  Whose judgment thou must soon abide ;
Thy blacken'd soul below will rove,
  In frightful torture far and wide.
Then wilt thou curse the deeds which gave
  The soul such agony to bear ;
'Tis easy now the thoughts to brave,
  And keep the mind above such fear.

My father's blood still dyes that hand,
  And now the son awaits his fate ;
Thy name's accursed in the land ;
  Thou turn'st thy people's love to hate.
Yet, if my blood will pleasure give,
  Thou art my King, I will obey ;
I would not for the future live,
  To view thy crimes from day to day.
So do with me whate'er thou wilt,
  Add but another to the roll ;
And for the blood that will be spilt,
  I ask forgiveness for thy soul."

The youth there stands, so calm, so meek,
  Awaiting now his horrid doom,
That tears are furrowing many a cheek,
  As silence once more rules in gloom.

Hark ! swells the King's voice on the air ;
  In angry words his wrath is spent ;
They wait—his orders but to hear,
  And give their general assent.

"Good citizens ! ye have just heard,
  This daring youth speak words to me,
Which, though he lacks the wise man's beard,
  Proclaim at death my destiny.
I am your King and Emperor,
  And I as such will speak to you.
This youth has ventured to incur
  My anger, which he soon will rue.
Is it for him to talk and prate
  About the ways of wrong and right ?
Is it for him to tell my fate—
  I, whom your gladiators fight ?

"Nay, nay," they cry ; "we'll have him die ;
  Our Emperor is brave and good :"
How often had the public eye
  Beheld him shed his noble blood.

Commodus smiles, and bows his head ;
  He knows his craft has gain'd the day,
For though his presence gives them dread,
  Their anger sometimes clouds his way.

"Stand forth! bold Lucian," quoth he ;
  "And hear the doom that thou hast sought ;
I'll give thee yet the chance to free
  Thyself within yon noted court.

We have a lion in a cage,
  A noble beast for thee to try ;
Both he and thee a war shall wage,
  To prove thine own fair destiny.
What say you now my subjects bold ?
  Is this not justice in good sooth ?
A holiday for young and old,
  To see this prophesying youth."

A lusty shout proclaim'd assent,
  And thus the youth was led away ;
Until the time of the event,
  Should prove the victor in the fray.

    *   *   *   *   *

A godly pile, a sacred heap,
  The ruins of a temple great,
Where ancient splendours calmly sleep—
  A monument of priestly state.
The moon shines o'er the godly mass,
  And penetrates it's mystic shades ;
The gentle wind is heard to pass
  In whispers through the collonades,
And by the moon's e'erguiding ray,
  A form is seen to flitter by
And pass beneath the column'd way
  That towers above majestic'ly.
Not long to wait, the form appears—
  Not one but two we now behold ;
A maiden fair bedew'd with tears,
  A youth whose form is tall and bold.
The maiden's voice, so sad, so sweet,
  Breaks through the silence reigning there,
As, falling at her lover's feet,
  She begs his help in her despair.

"Oh! brave Ignatius," she cried,
  "Thy noble heart will soothe my woe ;
What will I do if Lucian dies ?

My brother's blood, must—shall not flow ;
You, of Quintilian descent,
Have suffered much from this dark King ;
If your great name could but prevent
This deed of blood, this monstrous thing.
Give me thy help, oh ! noble youth,
To raise remonstrance deep and loud,
And save him from the lion's mouth
And hungry gaze of gibing crowd."

She gently takes her lover's hand,
And fondly gazes on his face ;
And thus one minute do they stand,
Until his answer fills the space.

" My fair beloved, " answers he ;
" Could I but raise the public voice,
How happy would your lover be,
How quickly would his heart rejoice.
I am too young to try the plan ;
The people would but scorn my speech,
And tell me I'm a beardless man,
Too ignorant to prate and preach. "

" Alas ! too true, " the maiden cries,
And leans her hand upon his arm ;
Yet there is something in her eyes
Which speaks of some great conqu'ring charm.

" I'll see the King to-morrow morn,
And beg the life so dear to me ;
My gentle voice he will not scorn,
And he'll give me his liberty. "

With flashing eyes, the lover starts,
A frown contracts his noble brow ;
And through his frame a passion darts,
Absent before, but present now.

" Vituria !" the youth commands,
" Thou shalt not seek the King to see ;
Thy virtue in those bloodstain'd hands
Would change into impurity.
Depend upon thy lover's might ;
Thy brother shall by me be sav'd,

For though he'll picture in the fight,
    The lion shall by me be brav'd.

She draws his head close to her own
    And kisses him with loving pride,
Which quickly clears away the frown,
    Causing the passion to subside.
Yet soon another cloud is seen,
    To darken o'er that lovely face,
As in the moonlight so serene,
    Their forms still haunt the sacred place.

" Ignatius, what wouldst thou do,
    To give my brother back his life ?
Do nothing that this heart will rue,
    Oh ! pray not enter in the strife. "
" Nay, nay, there reigns a God above,
    To help me in my strategy ;
You still shall have a brother's love,
    To bless our happy unity. "

And silence reigns once more around,
    Those voices die upon the wind :
The dew that falls upon the ground,
    Wipes out the secret left behind.
And so we leave this sacred spot,
    Awaiting but the coming day ;
Imagining the victim's lot,
    Dependent on the coming fray.

     ❋   ❋   ❋   ❋   ❋

What does that mighty circle mean,
    Tow'ring above the court beneath,
Where hungry animals are seen,
    Awaiting but the call of Death,
Oh ! what a multitude is there,
    Who gaze in eagerness below :
Oh ! if the King would but appear,
    To open there and then the show.
Hark ! murmurs choke the atmosphere ;
    At last, their Emperor has come ;
They greet him with a mighty cheer,
    That floats along the heav'nly dome.

Unto his throne he makes his way,
  Where profligates around him stand ;
He gives the order of the day,
  And smiles while issuing his command.

Out from a dungeon, dim and drear,
  The youthful Lucian is brought ;
His countenance is free from fear,
  As forth he comes into the court.
His right hand grasps a glitt'ring sword,
  His left hand firmly grasps the shield ;
They give him not a cheering word,
  They know that he will have to yield.
No cry of pity greets his form,
  As boldly standing on his ground,
They wait impatient for the storm,
  Eager to hear another sound.
'Tis heard at last, so low, so deep,
  Like rolling thunder from afar ;
And forth the brute is seen to creep,
  From out its dim and dreary lair.
Straight to the youth it makes its way,
  Pacing the ground with crafty tread ;
The silence of that concourse gay,
  Is by their expectation fed.
There, crouching low upon the ground,
  With sweeping tail and flashing eyes.
The beast prepares the fatal bound,
  Which gallantly the youth defies.
At last, at last, the spring is made,
  Yet look ! the lad is sound and free ;
He wields aloft the keen-edged blade,
  And strikes for life and liberty.
The sword sends forth a rapid gleam,
  And passes thro' the lion's side ;
The crimson blood is seen to stream,
  From out the wound a rushing tide.
The youth prepares to smite again,
  His sword is lifted for the blow ;
But crash—the paw breaks it in twain,
  He's at the mercy of the foe.
A piercing shriek breaks on the air,
  " False ! False ! Ignatius ! " is heard ;

Yet ere that last word of despair
    That mighty multitude is stirr'd.
A deadly shaft with light'ning speed,
    Gives back to Lucian his life ;
He, from the wounded brute is freed,
    Some other hand joins in the strife.

Look, see, Commodus, how he frowns,
    But hark! his voice sounds terribly.
" My citizens, a thousand crowns
    To him who brings that man to me. "

They know not whence the weapon came,
    They hardly saw the fatal dart,
Until the object of its aim
    Lay pierc'd in death, right through the heart.
He bids another sword be giv'n,
    Another lion to be freed ;
He scorns to have the youth forgiv'n
    Until his gallant form shall bleed.
Again he meets the lion's eye,
    Again we hear that cry of woe :
Again a shaft is seen to fly,
    And overpower the mighty foe.
The people raise a joyful cry,
    This sight was never seen before ;
The Emperor moves angrily
    And shouts his orders out once more.

This time six brutes, instead of one,
    From out their dens are seen to start ;
Yet as they fiercely to him run,
    Each one is pierced through the heart.
Again the shout, once more the frown,
    But all the lions now are dead ;
Commodus rises from his throne,
    The people's joy is turned to dread.
He from a soldier takes a sword,
    And goes into the court beneath ;
They wait with eagerness his word,
    And gaze there with abated breath.

" Some daring hand, " he cries aloud,
    " Has sav'd this malefactor's life ;

Instead of lying in his shroud,
　He lives uninjured in the strife.
Behold, if that one dares to give
　A helping hand to save him now,
Then by the gods, I'll let him live,
　And ye shall see, I'll keep my vow."
Yet as the sword is seen to flash,
　Determined that the blood be spilt,
Another shaft is seen to crash
　The threat'ning weapon to the hilt.

Deaf'ning the roars which shake the air,
　When they behold the youth is free ;
Commodus gives an angry glare,
　Yet gives to him his liberty.

And if the court-we could but search,
　We'd find a den in which we see,
Ignatius, upon his perch,
　Smiling in grim security.

We leave the lovers to their joy,
　We will not touch that sacred shrine ;
We would not now their peace destroy,
　But leave them to their love divine.

The Passing Bell.

FROM day to day a bell is heard,
Solemn and sad, with measur'd toll :
Alas ! its muffl'd peal to death
(Weird in its gloomy length and pow'r)
Casts o'er the multitude a spell
Which numbs each beating heart with fear
Or woe, and hauntings of the grave.
Behold ! within our peaceful homes
Creeps noiselessly a spectral form,
Spreading, with unrelenting hand,
Cold and damp, and foul disease.
Vain seem the efforts made to check
Its onward course.　It baffles all,
And moves in mystic silence on
Where'er it lists.

F

JOHN EMMET, F.L.S.

BY GEORGE ACKROYD, J.P.

———

JOHN EMMET was born at Final Royd House, Birkenshaw, in 1822. He was educated at Elam's Academy, Birstall. About thirty years ago he removed to Boston Spa, at which charming locality he has resided, more or less, ever since. When quite a youth the poetic faculty strongly developed itself in his nature, and he commenced contributing dainty gems to several of the principal Yorkshire papers. A passion for Botany, Antiquities, Conchology, Gardening and collecting Flint Implements also appeared, and articles from his pen on these and kindred subjects appeared in the *Bradford Observer* and other publications many years since. Mr. Emmet has also contributed to the *Archæological Journal*, *The Naturalist*, *Chambers's Journal*, *Science Gossip* and numerous other leading magazines from the *Standard* downwards. He was elected a Fellow of the Linnæan Society in 1885. It is much to be regretted that Mr. Emmet has never yet issued his poems in book form. He says in a letter received lately, " I have many volumes of MSS., but I never had pluck to publish." In 1878 he visited Italy and was introduced to Pope Leo XIII. and Victor Hugo. Among other men he has had the privilege of knowing and associating with are Wordsworth, Hartley Coleridge, James Montgomery, Charles Waterton and P. J. Bailey. Mr. Emmet was also intimately acquainted with many of the characters in Charlotte Brontë's " Shirley"; four or five of them were his personal friends. A distant relative of his is John Strange Winter, whose aunt, his uncle married. Says Miss E. Helen Barlow, of Bury, in "North Country Poets," " He (Mr. Emmet) enjoys his *otium cum dignitate*, and has not an enemy in the world. He lives in a house smothered with roses, and filled with old china bric-a-brac, antiquarian and other curiosities, as Waugh would say, 'crom full of ancientry and Roman hawpennies,' and books and pictures old and new. He leads a cultured life, varied by travel, retaining his intellectual tastes in all their freshness, enjoys life and his churchwarden pipe, and is never better pleased that when offering hospitality to old friends of similar tastes; and indeed, with his quaint, happy way of looking at things, his inexhaustible fund of apt anecdote and vast general information, a more entertaining companion or genial host would be hard to find."

His love for every living creature wins in return the fearless confidence of all animals, who seem at once to recognise him as a friend.

In Mr. Emmet's neighbourhood he is regarded as a sort of walking encyclopedia, and whenever coins or trophies, shells or rare flowers, curious stones, or old books are discovered, he is supposed to know all about them and name them as did Adam in Eden."

The poems appended will amply prove Mr. Emmet's right to a prominent place among the Spen Valley Poets, and though he is now far removed from the locality, thirty years of his youth spent in and near Birkenshaw always lends to his present day life a kindly and tender recollection. "Golden Stairs" is reprinted from a leaflet possessed by the late Abraham Holdroyd, and which appeared in the "Bradfordian." It has been reprinted many times.

Pessimist and Optimist.

A True Story of a worthy Spen Valley Couple.

OLD Billy Buttons went to bed
    And never slept a wink;
Bad debts, green harvests ruled his head,
    He could do nought but think.

His old wife Dolly slumbered nigh
    As he rolled round and swore;
Oft in his heart he wondered why
    She could both sleep and snore.

So passed the night—a restless toss—
    But Dolly slept right through;
Then Billy in the morn waxed cross
    And crowed, like Doodle Doo!

Chuck, chuck! I never slept the night,
    I saw the rising sun;
"And didst thee earn a shilling by't,"
    Clucked Dolly, when he'd done.

Old Dolly did the best she could,
  And prophesied the best ;
But Billy floundered in the mud,
  And much mud spoiled his rest.

Then Billy looked at puss and pug,
  On cushions by the fire ;
"They have no markets, and they're snug,
  What more can hearts desire ?

And Dolly, why can't thee and me,
  Live like our dog and cat ?"
" Tie 'em together, lad," laughed she,
  "Thoul't see what they'll be at ! "

Now, Dolly Buttons took life well—
  Just loved it as it flies—
Old Billy always lived in Hell,
  Dolly in Paradise !

The Evolution of Love.

TELL me how love begins to grow—
In callow youth the seed we sow,
  And culture well with hopes and fears ;
Straightway its blossoms burst and blow
Like fiery fireworks all aglow—
  O, for those firework, fiery years,

When love was young and skies were blue,
All lies untold and all hearts true,
  And chivalrous friend and lover—
When every sheep immaculate
Was bleating to its amorous mate,
  Knee-deep in verdurous clover.

Well—still love grows—from youth to eld,
The mightiest tree man ever beheld,
  Since first in Paradise planted—
Thereto flock all the pretty doves
From the whole world to coo their loves,
  And every branch is haunted.

O, wondrous tree of most renown,
No Hercules may hew thee down,
    Immortal, universal tree—
If once thy flowers forget to blow,
Farewell to everything below,
    And Heaven would perish without thee.

So boys and girls, still cultivate
The ancient tree with hearts elate,
    Bless it in shade and shower and shine,
And take through life ambrosial sips
From its ripe flowers nectareous tips,
    Thus Eve and Adam lipped its wine.

Learning from Nature.

DRINK of the alpine stream,
    Eat of the garner'd corn ;
Go lie on the summer sward and dream,
And fetch new light from the violet beam
    That brings the morn.

Sit in the moonlit tower,
    Sit when the night-bird sings,
And watch the bat to its breezy bower,
And the moth, as it folds in the folding flower
    Its amber wings.

Rise with the moorland bee,
    Sing with the mountain breeze,
And gather strength from the healthy sea,
And bring love and peace from the hawthorn lea
    And solemn trees.

Weep with the drops of dew,
    Laugh with the golden star,
Open your soul as wide as the blue,
And with granite old headlands climb, and view
    The lands afar.

Toil with the crater's glow,
    Play with the wild flower's crest,
Be firm and bold as the rocks below,
And as kind and calm as the arching bow
    On the storm-god's breast.

Search in the jewell'd mines,
　Stray on the coral strand,
Grow rich by the sapphire cloud that lines
The couch of the sun, when the monarch shines
　Adieu to land.

Love with the gentle birds,
　Praise with the hoar cascade,
And utter joy with the lambkin herds,
That bleat to their dams their musical words
　In the pine-wood's shade.

Dive into hidden caves
　Like the merman in the sea,
Swim with the nautilus over the waves,
And muse with the owlet among the graves
　Where dead men be.

Think with a hearty brain,
　Breathe with a joyous breath,
Let the snows bleach each innocent stain,
And the wild heart warm with a holy strain,
　That knows not death.

Feel with the smallest worm,
　Learn from the lowest clod,
Get truth in the flash of the lambent storm,
And beauty and good from every form
　That tells of God.

Golden Stairs.

THERE is a cottage by the stream,
　Whose thatch is near a century old,
'Tis never scorched with summer's beam,
　With winter's ice 'tis never cold—
I often watch them in and out
　The children and the good old pair,
For in that cot beyond a doubt,
　There is an unseen, golden stair.

Whilst sang the thrush one sultry night,
　Amongst the roses round the door,
They laid a gentle girl in white,
　I never heard or saw her more—

But those who watched her smile at last,
  And those who heard her latest prayer, ·
Aver, that up to heaven she passed,
  Passed upward by that golden stair.

An autumn morning, cool with mist,
  Brought its raw wind amongst the trees,
And just as God's new red light kist
  The frost-flowers from the lattices,
A boy lay on his sister's bed,
  He quite as gentle, cold and fair,
Some called it death—but he, when dead,
  Went upward by that golden stair.

And others ; some were in their prime,
  Just wedded when that thatch was new,
Went in and out a little time,
  Lived, loved, and lost, like me and you—
And went away, unseen by me ;
  They went, you need not ask me where,
They went where we oft wish to be,
  Right upward by that golden stair.

And now whilst pulling vernal flowers,
  And now while sings the same old thrush,
And now whilst fall the autumn showers,
  Upon the beaded hawthorn bush,
The loved ones left will gather round,
  Low listening to the dear old pair,
Who point them to each lowly mound,
  And point them to that golden stair.

You never saw that rosy cot,
  Or sunned yourself amongst its blooms,
Or knew the treasure it has got,
  The wealth that lines its cozy rooms ;
But you would see and hear them oft,
  Still climbing up if you were there,
And soon they all will be aloft,
  Gone upward by that golden stair.

Mayhap the cottage where you dwell,
  Is bright with bloom, and prankt with green,
And oh, if you would search it well,
  There may be golden stairs unseen,
For if to you the grace be given,
  To love the God who hears your prayer,
Be sure you have the road to heaven,
  Your cottage has the golden stair.

God Blesseth Everywhere.

THERE'S joy within the cottage door,
    And joy within the hall;
Joy for the rich and for the poor,
    For you, and me, and all.
God never stints the meed of bliss
    Nor deals too great a share;
But loves yon world, yet loveth this—
    God blesseth everywhere.

Whene'er I see a cottage rose
    Around the doorway creep;
Whene'er I see the deer-park close,
    The palace in its sleep,
I wonder do ye weep and sigh,
    Or are ye happy there;
And then I sing, and thus sing I—
    God blesseth everywhere.

And when I hear a grateful hymn
    Float down the river's tide;
Or see within the garden trim,
    Friends happy side by side,
I thank my loving God for what
    I hear and see so fair,
And hear and feel with praises that
    God blesseth everywhere.

O tenants of the hall or cot,
    Ye may have raven eyes,
Yet sigh for bliss that woos ye not,
    Or woo it till it flies;
Or ye may have no cherry cheek,
    And yet defy all care;
God heals the heart—it shall not break—
    God blesseth everywhere.

The birds laugh through the summer time
    In pleasure on the trees,
And every harebell rings a chime
    Of music for the bees;
The honey-bee on humming wing
    Goes roving here and there,
And sings with every living thing—
    God blesseth everywhere.

The clouds lie dreaming on the deep,
  All in a joyous dream ;
The merry stars do never sleep,
  So bright with love they seem ;
'Tis sung by valley, plain and hill,
  Through ocean, earth, and air ;
Ye may be happy if ye will—
  God blesseth everywhere.

We Cannot Stay.

WE cannot stay, said the winter stars,
We shall set to-night, to-morrow to rise
Upon other worlds and other eyes ;
  Gaze fondly and well on our glorious light,
  For our silver lamps must go out to-night :
    We cannot stay.

We are hurrying on from our mother hills,
Said the little springs ; we shall soon be gone ;
Drink a long draught as we hurry on ;
  With the falling eve we shall join the river,
  To-morrow be lost in the sea for ever :
    We cannot stay.

We cannot stay, said my petted flowers ;
Gay tendrils next year shall cover your door,
But we shall have fled to bloom no more ;
  Go gather some leaves to keep for our sake,
  For next year there shall be no leaves to take :
    We cannot stay.

I follow those stars said a dying child !
And all my hopes said, I follow those waves,
And they sleep like those flowers in perfumed graves ;
  And I heard them sing as I saw them flee,
  There's a better world for us and for thee :
    We cannot stay.

Changing friends of a changing world,
Keep heart !—we may love what we have loved best
In a changeless world, where all are blest ;
  Where only the sorrows that make us mourn,
  And only our sighs shall sigh in their turn :
    We cannot stay.

HARRIET GARSIDE.

By A. RAMAGE. M.D L.R.C.P. Edin.

LICENTIATE OF THE ROYAL COLLEGE OF SURGEONS,
EDINBURGH, AND OF THE FACULTY OF PHYSICIANS AND SURGEONS,
GLASGOW; FORMERLY ACTING SURGEON, BRADFORD
BOROUGH POLICE FORCE.

Miss HARRIET GARSIDE was born at Birkenshaw, November 11th, 1830. She has contributed poems for many years to the *Cleckheaton Guardian* and other papers, and has also issued several small booklets of verse, the titles of which are "Select Poems by Miss Harriet Garside. Birkenshaw," pp. 28, printed by Fearnley Brothers, of Adwalton. These were printed so that the proceeds from their sale might be given towards the building fund of the St. Paul's Church Sunday School, Drighlington. The second was also a 28 pp. pamphlet printed in 1882, by E. Mallinson, of Birstall, the proceeds of which were given in aid of a Bazaar held in St. Paul's Sunday School, Birkenshaw, on Easter Monday and Tuesday, ten years ago. This was entitled "A Selection of Poems." The third and last booklet was also issued for a similar laudatory purpose as the two former ones, at the beginning of last year. It was a 16 page one, with a title like its predecessors, and was printed by Mallinson & Son, of Birstall. Miss Garside possesses true poetic proclivities, and she is never so joyful as when jotting down jingling bits of rhyme—"even though they only please herself," as she says. She is a thorough Christian woman, always ready and willing to work in the cause of her Maker. Miss Garside was one of the first scholars in connection with St. Paul's Church Sunday School, Birkenshaw, and for more than fifty years she has retained her connection with the Church and Schools—at present being teacher to a large class of young women. Her jubilee connection with St. Paul's was celebrated a year or two ago, and this occasion was taken advantage of by her friends to present her with an illumin-

ated address, together with a purse of gold. Miss Garside has also
been the happy recipient of many other valuable presents, among
which may be mentioned a silver tea and coffee service, a beautiful
writing desk, and several richly bound Bibles and Prayer Books. Long
may she live to carry on her good work—all of which is done in a
quiet, unostentatious manner, yet brings forth abundant results.

St. Paul's Sunday School.

THIS festival day long remembered will be :
Of St. Paul's Sabbath School 'tis the first jubilee.
I reflect on the past both with smiles and with tears ;
I scarcely could think it was fifty long years

But change, busy change, has been hard at work here,
And friend after friend I have seen disappear ;
But others came forward their places to fill,
So this great work of mercy is carried on still.   •

But you, who with Sabbath School comforts are blest,
Have not known the trouble of making a nest ;
It is already made, by the kindness of friends,
But its future success on you greatly depends.

'Tis a work of importance, of patience, and care—
Needs a portion of time, wealth, labour, and prayer ;
Our fathers thought good such a plan to put forth,
And fifty years' use must have tested its worth.

It is where the Church nurses her girls and her boys—
A foretaste of bliss, are those Sabbath School joys ;
'Neath silvery locks we can sing to its praise,
That the sunshine of life are our Sabbath School days.

It has not all been sunshine, but sunshine and shade,
Since the foundation stone of St. Paul's School was laid ;
But this meeting to-day is sufficient to prove
God himself gives reward for the labour of love.

Where are my friends, unto me once so dear?
They are all old and gone while I still linger here;
Some are gone forth on duty, some sweetly at rest,
But the nursery business goes on in the nest.

The gems of society often have sprung
From those who were Sabbath School children when young;
The hope of the Church are its boys and its girls,
And the beauty of Heaven are those priceless pearls.

But why am I spared? perhaps in answer to prayer
The Lord has been pleased an old scholar to spare.
My teacher's advice I give freely to all—
Stand firm to your post; strive in harness to fall.

For your mark of esteem, God alone can repay;
I feel very thoughtful, yet thankful to day;
How different these times from our once humble lot;
But yet old acquaintance can ne'er be forgot.

Lines

ON THE WRECK OF ST. PAUL'S CHURCH, BIRKENSHAW,
MARCH, 1892.

THE home of my mother seems strange unto me,
Not a chip of church furniture here can I see;
The venerable walls are all naked and bare,
Desolation itself seems the ruling guest there.

The vestry, the organ, and seats are all fled,
And even the flags from the place where I tread,
The galleries and pillars are taken away,
And the clock in the tower has nothing to say.

But the faithful old bell with the greatest of care,
When the Sabbath comes round calls the children to prayer;
Though the mother is crippled and cannot give aid,
A substitute has for the dear ones been made.

I muse on the past as I stand gazing here,
But where are the friends unto me once so dear;
In this sweet little spot they have toil'd very hard,
Let us hope they are reaping the promised reward.

Old friends and their works are departed and gone,
Which were thought in their day to be second to none;
But the past has become a mere tale that is told,
And the modern design takes the place of the old.

'Tis surprising to think where the furniture stood,
As we view such large heaps of the broken-up wood;
Yet it all had a place in the dear house of prayer,
And many have felt it was good to be there.

The old grey stone walls seem to watch over those
Who are scatter'd around in their final repose;
But the names of the honour'd, the brave, and the just
Are cherish'd when they are asleep in the dust.

This dear sacred spot was my childhood's delight,
And I love it no less with my locks turning white;
Many changes have here taken place it is true,
But the greatest presents itself now to my view.

Lines

ON A DRAWINGROOM MEETING HELD IN OAKROYD HALL,
BIRKENSHAW, NOVEMBER 28, 1890.

As we wander along in the cold cheerless street,
What a number of waifs and strays we can meet;
They each had a mother indeed, but alas!
They chiefly belong to a very low class.

They perhaps are the issue of some once lov'd well,
Who have fallen in life, but why, we cannot tell;
They may deserve pity much greater than blame,
Were we left to ourselves we might soon do the same.

Some children must pilfer, or beg for their bread,
There is no other means by which they can be fed;
They also must bring a few coppers for beer,
Or expect from their parents a beating severe.

They are out in the snow with their bare little feet,
Unnoticed by those they may pass in the street;
They are dirty, and ragged, and tatter'd, and torn,
It seems almost a pity they ever were born.

Those desolate ones seek a place in the light,
Where they may take rest in the cold and dark night;
Perhaps under an arch, or the steps of some door
Is the only retreat of those wretchedly poor.

Shall those who are blest with their houses and lands,
Fail to take up such cases as these in their hands;
Those little street outcasts are objects of love,
Whose names are recorded in mansions above.

They have got souls and bodies, can both laugh and sing,
And their shrill little voices can make the streets ring;
But who can rejoice when despis'd and forlorn,
And feel the keen piercings of hunger's sharp thorn.

Then is it a crime to be poor? it is not,
For Jesus himself honour'd poverty's lot;
To rescue those children from ruin is just,
The talent Christ's followers hold in their trust.

For the time is approaching, 'tis fast on its way,
When the streets shall be fill'd with the children at play;
And those who are blest with wealth, talent or skill,
Are appointed by God his decree to fulfill.

Kind Words.

Kind words can never die 'tis true,
They fall and soften as the dew;
They cheer, revive, and beautify,—
Kind words are things that never die.

When all around is cold and dull,
And sorrow fills the heart quite full,
Kind words will rend those waves apart,
And find an entrance to the heart.

Kind words are like the distant chime,
They sweep along the sands of Time;
Those sounds will reach from shore to shore
When lips that spoke them are no more.

Kind words are cheap—yet very dear,—
They smite the rock, and draw the tear,
Which bursts into a mighty flood,
And does mankind a power of good.

Like little seeds, kind words are sown,
Their places to the world unknown :
But in the season they will spring,
And fruit into perfection bring.

Kind words the feeble one will cheer,
Say to the brave one persevere ;
From them the faint take heart again,
And set to work with might and main.

Speak kindly, 'tis the gentle word,
That like a sharp two-edged sword,
'Twill but require one gentle touch,
Or it might wound the part too much.

Kind words, when dropt in memory's grave,
Will bloom upon the roaming wave,
And make the hero of the main
Think that he is at home again.

Kind words are sweet on every tongue,
And pleasant from both old and young:
Like sweet perfume they fill the air,
And scatter blessings everywhere.

Though toss'd about like thistle down,
They settle in a place unknown,
And in some unexpected spot
They spring a sweet Forget-me-not.

Kind words are like a magnet spell,
Whenever tried they answer well ;
Though at a very trifling cost,
Kind words are never, never lost.

Kind words the spirit will revive,
And keep the spark of life alive,—
Fed by the flame of love divine,
As lights in this dark world they shine.

Kind words when soft and sweetly said,
Are comforts on a dying bed :
O that their number might increase,
And make this world of war at peace,

Kind words can never drop in vain,
Though hidden they may long remain ;
Some foreign land may boast the fruit,
Which in its native soil took root.

Kind words are leaves upon that tree
Which brings forth fruit of sympathy ;
They cheer the young, support the old—
Of greater value far than gold.

Kind words are what the world approves,
And what the world's Creator loves.
Kind words, Oh ! let the echo fly,—
Kind words can never, never die.

Kind words are jewels set in fame,
And honours on the honour'd name ;
Kind words are pure and well refined,
Though few your words, let them be kind.

The Old Barren Tree.

A FIGURE, barren, bare and dry,
Stood pointing to the azure sky ;
It once could boast of beauties fair,
'Tis now an object of despair.

While all things round look'd fresh and gay,
Clad in the splendid robes of May,
Yet spring had no improvement made
In this tall object here display'd.

Its vacant stems are bare and cold,
And hence the tale of age is told ;
Its splendour is for ever o'er,
And perish'd to be seen no more.

Yet from this barren tree is heard
The lovely notes of some sweet bird ;
It seems to call attention where
We view the object with despair.

It once could boast the robe of Spring,
On well clad boughs the birds could sing ;
Its graceful branches I have seen
Array'd, as all its friends, in green.

Each Autumn turn'd the green leaves brown,
And bleak winds came and shook them down;
Cold Winter's hand shook dust of snow
Which rested on each graceful bough.

It brav'd the storms, and pass'd them by,
Embrac'd the light'ning from the sky ;
While many things found swift decay,
It rob'd each Spring and welcom'd May.

'Twas planted in the days of yore ;
The planter's name is known no more ;
And many have beheld that tree,
And shar'd the self-same fate as he.

Perhaps some will say, why view that tree ?
There's nothing striking there to see ;
Its better days are past and gone,
And bloom and beauty there is none !

'Tis even so, but, bear in mind,
It speaks a word to all mankind ;
Though long you live, and fair you bloom,
Decay at length will be your doom.

How many like this tree are found
But cumberers of the precious ground ;
While others bloom from year to year
They seem quite lifeless to appear.

While on this barren tree I gaze,
Let me reflect on bygone days :
I fear I shall be led to see
It very much resembles me.

On mercy's ground I still remain,
And trust that I shall bloom again
Where nature will no more decay,
But all the seasons bloom as May.

G

REV. W. M. HEALD, M.A. M.D.

By J. A. ERSKINE STUART, L.R.C.P. L.R.C.S. Edin.

AUTHOR OF "THE BRONTE COUNTRY"; "THE LITERARY
SHRINES OF YORKSHIRE"; FELLOW OF THE SOCIETY OF
ANTIQUARIES, SCOTLAND.

THE REV. WM. MARGETSON HEALD, M.A. Cantab, and M.D. Edin., was the son of John Heald, farmer and maltster, of Heald's House, Dewsbury Moor, where he was born towards the close of last century. His father and four other Johns were styled the "four wise Johns of Dewsbury," because they caused a survey of the township to be taken which was afterwards squashed by the Wakefield bench of magistrates. As a boy he attended the old grammar school at Batley, and being destined for the medical profession pursued his studies at

HEALD'S HOUSE, DEWSBURY MOOR.

Edinburgh University, where the celebrated Brunonian controversy was in full blast. John Brown, the author of the "Brunonian Theory of Medicine," which was aimed primarily at the indiscriminate use of the bleeding lancet, was a native of Berwickshire brought up in great poverty. Originally destined for the Church, he was attracted to the study of medicine by being asked to translate a Latin medical thesis into English. His excellent knowledge of classics brought him under the notice of Archibald Cullen, who at this time was bringing forward a theory of medicine of his own founded on Hoffman's nervous theory of disease. After graduating as M.D. he became a bitter opponent of his late patron Cullen, and finally promulgated what is now styled the Brunonian theory of medicine, which, without doubt, has been helpful in bringing to pass a revolution in the treatment of disease. Young Heald was an admirer of Brown's and wrote a poem entitled the "Brunoniad" in praise of the latest views which were creating a perfect tempest among the faculty of the day.

Heald also studied under the celebrated John Hunter, of London, and ultimately graduated as M.D. at Edinburgh University. He then settled in Wakefield as a surgeon, but, like Oliver Goldsmith, he was

HEALD'S HALL, LIVERSEDGE.

not successful in attracting patients. It seems he had only one. Disgusted with his want of success he set about looking for another calling, and his brother John, a banker's clerk in London, defrayed all his expenses while resident at Cambridge preparing for Holy Orders. After his ordination he was licensed to the curacy of Birstall; in place of Reuben Ogden, deceased. At the time Heald came to Birstall it was a large undivided parish containing a population of 25,000 souls. He was presented to the vicarage in 1801.

Heald is an example of the versatile popular clergyman, who, although thoroughly in earnest about his Master's business, is yet able to devote his attention to the education of the young and to literary pursuits. The main features of his life ought to be an encouragement to present day country parsons who are often, no doubt, apt to feel that

their surroundings are prosaic and uninteresting, and who find it easier
to sink down into a gloomy round of routine duties than to brace
themselves for the uphill fight against apathy and worldly mindedness.
There is nothing like a hobby for everyone. The man who stinks of
the shop when he mixes with his fellows is a nuisance in society. The
hobby may be a change of work, but the busy man is the man to do
any work well), and all work and no play make Jack a dull boy. When
William Heald left Cambridge he brought two pupils with him who
afterwards rose to be dignitaries of the Church. Thomas Musgrave,
Bishop of Hereford, and afterwards Archbishop of York, and his
brother, who became Archdeacon of Halifax, were the lads.

BIRSTALL CHURCH.

Heald's services as an educationist were not confined to the instruction of the pupils of wealthy parents, but it was his wont to
instruct the older lads of the parish at night schools held twice a week,
in the "three R's," and such other branches they wished to be taught.
Again, during his vicariate, Sunday schools became a power in the
parish.   Hitherto, they had been parochial institutions, and the
children attended Church and Wesleyan Chapel alternately. He as-
sociated them with the Church, and by his week-day secular instruction, managed to gain a hold which has since been kept up. In
"Shirley," the school feast at Briarfield (Birstall) will be remembered,
with its remarkable mingling of word painting and West Riding
dialogue. During Heald's term of office great strides were made in
planting new churches in this thickly-populated and rapidly-increasing
parish.

The following specimen of Dr. Heald's verses, is to be found in a volume of sermons of his which were published in 1877. Following a discourse on the horrors of war, founded on the words, "Come, O breath, and breathe upon those slain," preached after the glorious victory of Waterloo, we find the accompanying lines, headed "Waterloo. Composed for the occasion, by the Rev. W. M. Heald."

Not only did Heald carry on with so much energy these various employments, but, in addition, he also ministered to the bodies of his parishioners, and was thus a valuable home medical missionary in this extensive parish. He is singled out for remembrance as an example of a many-sided character who was a blessing to his day and generation. He died January 13th, 1837, aged 70 years, and was succeeded in the vicarage by his son, William Margetson Heald, M.A., Trinity College, Cambridge, who had been curate of the parish from 1827 to 1831.

Waterloo.

O! BREATHE, upon the soldier's grave,
　In solemn dirge, the grateful strain—
Pay life's last honours to the brave,
　To guard their injured country slain.

Beneath a foreign soil they sleep:
　Their dauntless breasts now burn no more;
For them their widow'd partner's weep,
　For them their orphan babes deplore.

O! give them pity's soothing tear,
　Fond charity's indulgent boon,
Do thou, mid'st woe's deep night, appear,
　Be thou fair joy's benignant moon.

Britain, to poverty consign'd,
　Leave not thy warrior's humble home;
For round thy envied brows they bind,
　Bright laurels of unfading bloom.

Our prayers, Great God of nature, hear
　Quench thou the blaze of hostile ire;
And break the bow, and snap the spear,
　And war's red chariot burn with fire.

O! bid the soldier's blood-stain'd hands,
　Forsake the sword, and ply the oar;
While peace her sheltering wings expands,
　From realm to realm, from shore to shore,

Moscow.

The Poem on Moscow, which we give in full, first appeared in 1813. It was printed in pamphlet form by Ridgway, Piccadilly, London.

I. 1.

YET, Britannia, yet rejoice;
Lash'd by rolling storms of war,
From thy foam-clad rocks afar,
　Raise thy triumphant voice.
#"Son of radiant morning," cry,
"Vanquish'd art thou, fallen from high!
Thou that mad'st the nations bow,
Is thy martial pomp brought low?
Kingdoms trembled at thy frown,
Warrior, are thy hosts cut down?"
　Midst the battle's madding roar,
Since to joy proud conquest calls,
Prostrate, when the foeman falls,
　Bid the song of triumph soar.

I. 2.

　Thus the Muse awakes her fire;
Calls the queen of circling deeps,
While, with pausing hand, she sweeps
　Her long-forgotten lyre.
Though ignoble, bleak and poor,
Sweet is still a native shore.
Then what charms refulgent smile
When 'tis glory's fruitful isle?
When, amidst an abject world,
Freedom there her flag unfurl'd;
　Alfred filled a peerless throne,
Avon's bard and Milton sung,
Truth to light with Bacon sprung,
　Locke and wondrous Newton shone.

I. 3.

Behold, vindictive France, behold, in vain
　Thine arm is lifted and thy lightning flies;
Still safe amidst the desarts of the main,
　Thy rival rests and all thy threats defies.
Isaiah, chap. xiv.

O land! ere while aroused from slavery's thrall
And fill'd with Freedom's animating call,
Was it for this Oppression griev'd,
And, from its base, old empire heav'd?
Was it for this thy *dungeon fell?
For this thy hapless Lewis bled?
For this did sanguine torrents swell
When Paris mourn'd her heaps of dead?
Did all thy squadrons crowd the embattled field,
Rage ever fresh, amid the ceaseless fight,
Repel of Europe the collected might,
For Corsica the despots' rod to wield?
Not thus the sons of ancient days
Seiz'd the fair palm of endless praise;
Heroic Greece, majestic Rome,
Arose sublime, from servile gloom;
Arose, determined to be free,
And fix'd serene their star of liberty.
But, France, thy sons forego the claim,
They combat for another's fame,
And toil, assiduous toil, to spread,
War's bloody wreaths round proud ambition's head.

II. 1.

See where the vast Colossus stands,
While prostrate realms expectant gaze;
Surveys his congregated bands,
And bids ten thousand banners blaze:
" Not yet the victim of dismay,
And dares adventurous Russia disobey?
With wounds unheal'd already gor'd,
Again provoke th' avenging sword?"
Then hoarse the ponderous portal growls,
And forth the thundering cannon rolls,
'Tis all one universal jar;
Thick levell'd tubes promiscuous dash,
Steeds prance, and gleaming faulchions flash,
Dire prelude of prodigious war.

II. 2.

As rolls the swarming mass along,
It swells by tributary streams;

* The Bastile.

Earth groans beneath the endless throng,
  And rage his host resistless deems.
Yield, yield, affrighted Europe call'd ;
But Russia stood, resolv'd and unappall'd ;
Her martial prowler, stern, defied
The gallic vulture's ravenous pride—
The work begins, exulting France
Commands her myriads to advance.
They sweep the desolated plain ;
The ramparts yield, the foes retire,
Smolensko sinks in sheets of fire,
And horror hails her ample reign.

II. 3.

Where Moscow's glimmering domes ascend afar,
On Borodino's fatal soil,
Dread scene of Havock's most remorseless toil,
There stops the rushing tide of war.
There grimly meet confronting foes,
And there the ranks tumultuous close,
Immense rebellowing cannon pour,
From blazing mouths their iron shower ;
And thousands agonizing feel,
Dash'd through their hearts the murderous steel.
Shriek after shriek terrific swells,
Confusion shouts, and carnage yells :
'Tis Hell has disembogued her load,
And all her millions pour'd abroad,
So fierce, stupendous passion boils,
And faint, at length, indignant France recoils.
The sun of Austerlitz ! Napoleon, no—
That sun is sunk, in deep and awful gloom ;
It greets thee not, and conquest's purple plume
Here wafts no breeze to moderate thy woe.

III. 1.

Not that sun, 'tis Moscow's blaze,
  Rages, reddens, wraps, consumes ;
Deeds unheard thine eye surveys,
  Hallow'd fanes, imperial domes,
By their children's hostile hand,
  Whelm'd in conflagration dire ;

Powder, chief, and understand,
'Tis the blaze of boundless ire.
There thy batter'd legions dwell ?
Go, deluded hero, go :
Haughty, bold, infuriate fell,
Rage and Russia answer—no !

III. 2.

Wild, across her waste domain,
Then the Queen of Empire flew :
" Fame in unexampled strain,
Sounds, my sons, her trump to you.
Courage, 'tis your country's call ;
Gasping thousands yet must bleed.
O ! Pultowa's day recall,
Recollect the vanquish'd Swede :
Come, thy shafts, grim winter spread,
Aid, in fates vindictive hour :
And on Gallia's destined head,
All thy bellowing tempests pour."

III. 3.

Sublimely thron'd, far on the solid main,
Gigantic Winter heard, his arm laid bare ;
Unlock'd from shudd'ring frost th' enormous chain,
Stamp'd the mad fiend, and shook her icy hair,
Surge after surge, impetuous Boreas blew ;
On the wild blast, pale hideous Famine rode ;
Shot from her gloomy orbs, Distraction flew ;
Her shrivell'd arm Dismay hurl'd all abroad.
Immediate, nature's cheerful green
Became one white unvaried scene.
Arrested, pause the stony floods,
And bend, with snow, the humbled woods :
Howls, as they pass, the roaming bear,
With all her horrors, in the rear,
While Desolation wings her speed
And clasps her dreadful hands, and shouts—proceed.

IV. 1.

Of yore his pestilential breeze,
  As Israel's God* arous'd to blow,
Assyria's vaunting host to seize
  And lay her smother'd thousands low ;
So, onward dismal winter roll'd,
  And bade his bleak artillery roar;
And to desponding Gallia told
  Th' expected triumph all was o'er.
Not this the breeze, in vernal charms,
Gay Loire's voluptuous mead that warms;
  No more the bounding pulses beat :
From steed to steed, from man to man,
Frost's rapid bolts diffusive ran,
  And all exclaimed—retreat, retreat.

IV. 2.

Shrill rings the echoing trump, aloud
  The murmuring drum resounds, they move.
Before, behind, dire perils crowd,
  And all is hostile fate above ;†
Then swift the hoary veteran ran,
  And bade his shouting myriads hear ;
Waste all before the hurrying van,
  And hurl their thunders on the rear.
Black as the tempest o'er the field,
His steed the furious Cossack wheel'd,
And day and night gave no repose ;
While, through the drear expanse of air,
Sighed the sad Demon of Despair,
Big with immeasurable woes.

IV. 3.

Before mine eyes what scenes disast'rous spread !
  As falls the grass beneath the mower's blade,
So swift expands the region of the dead ;
  From hoast to hoast, the king of terror wades,
Mix'd with the murmurs of the moaning blast,
  The boundless clash of arms, incessant roars :
In vain, their eyes the piteous victims cast,
  Where absent friends repose, on native shores.

  * Kings, chap. xix.   † Kutuzoff.

Ah! to your country ye no more return,
No cheerful voice shall hail you welcome home ;
Nor o'er your graves afflicted kindred mourn :
Wild Scythia opes one vast, voracious tomb!
The pale and mangled spectacles of woe,
Wailful for you, compassion's chords I move ;
No hostile fate of yours aroused you—no—
You rush'd impell'd where're a tyrant drove !
To you the charms which win a sceptr'd brow,
Alas! what were they then, alas! what are they now.

V. 1.

High in th' historic fane display'd,
   Thy laurels, warlike Scythia, blaze ;
Since *Persia's lord, beneath thy blade,
   Fell, gash'd in war's tremendous maze ;
When not a cheek, with terror pale,
Return'd to tell the dismal tale.
Again, the mystic present true,
Another, by disaster knew ;
When back to Ister's stream return'd,
The remnant of his rescued host he mourned.

V. 2.

Alike, in conscious virtue bold,
   Her †bards their ancient fame unroll ;
Unsway'd by all seductive gold,
   And just and temperate of soul ;
Content with nature's simple store,
And rich, yea nobly rich, though poor.
For wealth, to sorid ore confin'd
Is vile, without the God-like mind :
Thence honour gems her blazing zone,
And genuine splendour decorates the throne.

V. 3.

Then hear, O Alexander, hear,
From thine the black pollution tear,
Deign from oppression's fangs to save,
Commiserate the vanquish'd brave.
See Poland stretch'd in abject woe,
Her tears, in burning currents flow,

Darius, King of Persia.   * Homer.

As the deep shafts transpierce her side,
And plunder rends her ancient pride.
On Heaven she calls in dark despair,
And vengeance waits the suppliant's prayer ;
Pours the full tempest from her urn,
And tells injustice it shall mourn.
Wash out the stains of Praga's gore,
Wrench from their grasp, with generous toil,
The sceptred robbers lawless spoil,
Proclaim to Poland that her woes are o'er.

VI. 1.

Xerxes warlike Greece invaded,
    Bade old ocean cease to foam, ·
Deem'd, with endless laurels shaded,
    To return triumphant home.
But with all his hosts surrounded,
    See, a paltry skiff enclose
Xerxes, pale, abash'd, confounded,
    When the sons of freedom rose.
Coward Xerxes, fac'd with danger,
    Danger's front recoil'd to see :
He to battle was a stranger,—
    But can Lodi's hero flee ?

VI. 2.

Flee, in lowly state disguising,
    Martial pomp, imperial pride !
Life's rejected boon despising,
    Nobly great Emilius died.
Scorning ere his fate to sunder,
    Bayard gave his generous gore ;
And amidst the battle's thunder,
    Glory wept o'er gallant Moore.
Led by an imperious master,
    To the dismal waste of woe.
From his soldier's dire disaster,
    Say, can Lodi's champion go ?

VI. 3.

Then here, fallen warrior, let the combat close,
And give the groaning world repose ;
And sheathe at length the slaughtering blade,
For, see, thy rapid course pourtray'd,
One dark, ensanguin'd map appears,
With parents drench'd, and widows' tears.
In torrents these around thee roar,
And all thy garments drop with gore.
Yea, thou hast pass'd thy blazing flight,
Like a red meteor of the night.
Once vaunted freedom's specious son,
Ambition's tempting trophies shine ;
And see the gaudy pageant won,
The gorgeous diadem is thine.
But what avails it, o'er thee when impends
That awful arm which lays the mighty low ;
Yet a short space, and all thy glory ends,
Then dark the future, all the past is woe.

VII. 1.

Drear is thy mien, despotic power,
　And poor are all thy vast domains,
Shades o'er thy purest sunshine lour,
　Health rolls no transport through thy veins.
No vernal breezes e'er control
Th' eternal winter of thy soul.
What can the servile herd impart,
To charm the haughty master's heart ?
Her wreaths tho' adulation wave,
The mind that there imperious swells,
Betrays the miser's vaunt, and tells
The despot is himself a slave.

VII. 2.

Alone in Freedom's fostering domes,
　Where streams of pure instruction flow,
Profuse, the human desart blooms,
　And virtues noblest scions grow.
Behold, the star-emblazon'd peer
Is man, and man the peasant there,

There shouting Commerce spreads her wings,
And Science there unlocks her springs,
And there th' unbending patriot sways ;
While through the gloom of mental night,
Keen Genius wings his soaring flight,
And all his corruscations blaze.

VII. 3.

How fair the auspicious lot where these combine !
My country ! is the blessing thine ?
Then guard, O guard the inestimable store,
Thy sage tny valiant sons obtain'd of yore.
And tell thy monarchs this to own,
The noblest gem that rays their envied crown.
Cleanse every stain, and every loss repair,
Bid thy fair pile in youth immortal glow,
The honour'd boon let all thy children share ;
Free as the bounding waves that round thee flow.
While thus thy liberal soul expands,
O win all hearts, unite all hands ;
Then let war around thee roar,
Filial fleets protect thy shore.
Deems th' invader thee his prize,
Fierce, thy martial millions rise,
Flame all eyes, and rush all hands,
Patriot banners to unfurl ;
And, on his devoted bands,
More than Russia's vengence hurl.

VIII. 1.

But come, O come, seraphic peace,
    Thy beams o'er woes bleak mountains throw,
Adorn thy climes, thy realms increase,
    And spread thy paradise below.
O make the spear and sword combine,
To plow the soil and prune the vine ;
And o'er the blood-discolour'd plain,
Rich harvests wave, of golden grain.
Thine is the lark-enliven'd morn,
The shepherd's pipe, the warbling grove,
The daisied mead, the lowing drove,
And thine fair plenty's bounteous horn.

Thee did not rapturous angels hail,
    When Bethlehem's babe appear'd, of yore ?
And wonder charm'd the passing gale,
    That man should harass man no more.
And art not thou to reign sublime,
·Beyond the fleeting realms of time ?
To ray with endless beams thy head,
When like a shadow earth is fled ?
O antedate th' immortal year,
Make passion's ruthless lion mild,
And, sportive, let the harmless child
Play with the asp, devoid of fear.

VIII. 3.

Drain the ocean to a rill,
Then shall Passion's pulse be still ;
Teach the rugged rock to feel,
Man shall drop the ensanguin'd steel ;
Make the tempest cease to blow,
He shall learn himself to know.
Let, great Creator, Thy paternal care,
    By Reason's beam, by Revelation's blaze.
Enough has given for erring man to share,
    To light his path, attract his solemn gaze,
Twin suns, to these her bosom conscience turns,
    And warns the soul to lend a faithful ear.
And mark the maze which heedless Folly spurns,
    Beyond the grave where mightier worlds appear.
Mark the dread hour, obedient to their doom,
When teeming earth, and ocean's ample womb,
Shall hear, shall heave, and pour forth all their slain.
When war's pale victims, from their silent beds,
Shall start, shall gaze, shall lift their wond'ring heads
And glow with joy, or agonize with pain.
Where is thy pomp, abandom'd vice, say where ?
'Tis Virtue's robe alone, which clothes the naked there.

POLLARD HALL, GOMERSAL.—THE RESIDENCE OF HERBERT KNOWLES.

HERBERT KNOWLES.

BY THE REV. R. V. TAYLOR, B.A. F.R.H.S.

VICAR OF MELBECKS, RICHMOND; AUTHOR "LEEDS WORTHIES,"
"THE CHURCHES OF LEEDS," "YORKSHIRE
ANECDOTES," ETC., ETC.

THE genius that in Knowles did brightly bloom,
    Was early snapped by Death's relentless wind ;
But though his ashes lie within the tomb—
    A name immortal he has left behind !
A name unsullied by the taint of sin—
    A name made lustrous by his heaven-sent power,
A name that others strive in vain to win—
    A name all fraught with poesy's rich dower!
How sad to think his weakly frame gave way,
    Just when his dawn rose radiant in the east,
How sad to think the noontide of his day
    Was scarcely reached ere his young life had ceased !
Yet why muse thus ? why heave the heartfelt sigh ?
He is not dead, and he can never die !

                                        EDITOR.

THIS extraordinary youth owes to a single composition of acknowledged
excellence a place among the poets of this country, from which no
accident is likely to remove him. He is said to have been born at
Gomersal in 1797 or 1798. His family was well connected in the commercial world, but the children, including at least our author and two
brothers—one of whom was the late Mr. C. J. Knowles, Q.C.,—were
early left orphans and almost destitute. Young Herbert was destined
for the ledger in a merchant's counting house at Liverpool, but the
drudgery of the desk was so little suited to the turn and temperament
of his mind that, by a series of providential circumstances, he ultimately
became placed in the celebrated Grammar School of Richmond in his
native county. To enable our author to attend this school a subscrip-
tion of £20 a year was made on condition that his friends should con-
tribute £30 more. Whilst at this celebrated school he evinced powers
of no ordinary kind, including that poetical talent of which such an
affecting and elegant memorial exists in the stanzas we have before
alluded to, and which we quote.

II

When he quitted Richmond his friends were unable to advance
any more money towards his education. To help himself, therefore,
he wrote a poem of considerable length, and sent it to Dr. Southey,
with a history of his case, and asked permission to dedicate it to the
Laureate. Southey, finding the poem "brimful of power and promise,"
made enquiries of Herbert's instructor, and received the highest
character of the youth. He then answered Knowles's application,
entreated him to avoid present publication, and promised to do better
than receive the dedication. He subscribed at once £10 per annum
towards the failing £30, and procured similar amounts from Mr.
Rogers and Lord Spencer. On receiving the news of his good fortune,
young Knowles wrote to his protector a letter remarkable for much
more than the gratitude which pervaded every line. He remembered
that Kirke White had gone to the university countenanced and sup-
ported by patrons, and that to pay back the debt he owed them, he
wrought day and night, until his delicate frame gave way and his life
became the penalty of his devotion. Knowles felt that he could not
make the same desperate efforts, and deemed it his first duty to say so.
He promised to do what he could, assured his friends that he would
not be idle, and that if he could not reflect upon them any extraordinary
credit, he would certainly do them no disgrace.

Preparatory to being removed to Cambridge, he was placed under
a kind and able instructor, but within two months after writing the
letter to Southey, the hopes which this ingenious youth had excited, and
to some extent gratified, were extinguished by his severe illness and
sudden death, at Gomersal, on February 17, 1817, aged 19 years. He
left behind him a manuscript volume of poems, the earliest of which
was printed in the *Literary Gazette* in 1824, pp. 58-9; but neither that
nor any of the others are at all comparable with the verses we give.
They were composed by Knowles in the churchyard at Richmond, on
October 7th, 1816, and are printed in the "History of Endowed
Grammar Schools," by Carlisle, under the head of Richmond.
Montgomery, the Christian poet, said of them :—"They ought to
"endear the memory of the author; truly he built a monument more
"durable than brass in composing these casual lines with little pros-
"pect of pleasing anybody but himself and a circle of juvenile friends."
The reader will remember that they are the verses of a youth of 17,
and will then judge what might have been expected from one who was
capable of writing with such strength and originality upon so trite a
subject.

In reply to the above, "Junius of Gomersal," writes to say " that
having, through the kindness of a member of the family from which
the poet was descended, as well as some small researches of my own,
become possessed of a little information on the subject, I determined

to endeavour to satisfy the curiosity of your readers. I was therefore pleased to see the very interesting account of the poet furnished by Dr. Forshaw, as besides giving me some information I needed, in order to give more accurate sequence to the facts I had gathered, it ministered to my natural indolence by saving me the pains of writing a detailed account. However, as I think there are several slight errors in Dr. Forshaw's narrative, which it may be as well to correct once for all, and the account of the poet's boyhood is a little incomplete, I think some amplification of the previous note might be of interest to your readers. In the first place, Herbert Knowles was born, not in 1798, but on the 30th of September, 1797, and not at Gomersal, but near Huddersfield, although he was educated at Gomersal, and died there. This mistake, which also occurs in Cudworth's 'Round about Bradford,' &c., is more important than it seems at first sight. Gomersal, after all, cannot boast of having produced this remarkable youth, but can only claim the secondary honour of having helped to form his early impressions. The error may have arisen from the fact that his brother having been born in that year (December 29th), though he too was born near Huddersfield, as was also the third brother, George. Another brother, Lionel Phillips, and a sister, Elizabeth, were born at Cheapside, London, whither the family removed. In 1805, James Knowles, the father of the children died, and as they had previously lost their mother they were left in the charge of different uncles and aunts. According to my information, Herbert fell to the share of an uncle in London, who wished to place him in business, but as this would leave Gomersal very little part indeed in him, I prefer to follow the account given in 'Round about Bradford,' and believe that before going to the uncle in London he lived with his aunt, Mrs. Phillips, of Pollard Hall, and from there attended Mr. Horsfall's School at Gomersal Hall. If this be accepted, we must admit the report also mentioned in 'Round about Bradford,' that, with the other boarders of the school, Herbert attended at the old Red Chapel, Cleckheaton, and at times delivered a short address during the interval between the services; though it would not be surprising if, in the course of further researches, it should be discovered that confusion had here arisen between him and the embryo Q.C. From our poet's letter to Southey we gather that he made no acquaintance with classical or mathematical literature at Gomersal Hall, but I have no information as to the conduct and mode of instruction in the school. Perhaps some of the readers of the *Guardian* might know something about it. It was the uncle in London, I believe, who wished to place Herbert in business, but he did not like the idea. He went from London to Canterbury, and there became acquainted with the Dean, Dr. Andrews, who took a great fancy to him, and exerted his influence successfully to gain him admission into the excellent school at Richmond, where, under the tuition of Canon Tate, whom Southey designated as 'a good and able man,' he stayed for two years. In the letter which he wrote to Southey, a copy of which is now before me, he writes thus of his life at Richmond:—'Out of that time during three months and two long vacations I have made but a retrograde course; during the remaining part of the time having nothing to look forward to, I had nothing to exert myself for, and wrapped in visionary thoughts and immersed in cares and sorrows peculiarly my own, I was diverted from the regular pursuit of those qualifications which are requisite for University distinctions.' Dr. Forshaw explained the circumstances

THE OLD RED CHAPEL, CLECKHEATON.

under which the poet was entered at St. John's College, Cambridge, also referring to the sad event which so rudely checked this promising career just when the clouds seemed to be dispersing. To this we may add, that he was buried at (I think) the Independent Chapel, Heckmondwike."

"Since the article on this talented youth appeared in the *Guardian* I have been requested by a firm of publishers to edit for them a volume of poetry, with biographical sketches, relating to authors who have published volumes of poems or otherwise made a local name, by writing and publishing their effusions in the press of Cleckheaton and the district immediately surrounding. Gomersal will be included, and I am therefore anxious that not the slightest error should occur in the facts relative to Herbert Knowles. I should like 'Junius' to inform me what facts he has to bear out his statement that Knowles 'was born near Huddersfield, on the 30th September, 1797.' To my mind 'near Huddersfield' is very indefinite, and I should much like some definite information on this point. The following authorities say 'Herbert

Knowles was born at Gomersal in 1798 :' ' Saturday Magazine ' 1836 ; 'Newsam's Poets of Yorkshire,' 1845 ; 'Grainge's Poets and Poetry of Yorkshire,' 1868 ; Cudworth's ' Round about Bradford,' 1876 ; Holroyd's ' Bards of Yorkshire,' 1873 ; Taylor's ' Leeds Worthies,' 1865 ; Carlisle's ' History of Endowed Grammar Schools'; 'Gentleman's Magazine '; Nicholl's ' Literary Illustrations'; and Schroeder's 'Annals of Leeds.' It will thus be seen that ' Junius ' has to ' prove incorrect ' the statement of the above historians. I was not only pleased but much interested to read his account of Knowles, and trust he will be able to settle satisfactorily the disputed date."

THE OLD UPPER CHAPEL, HECKMONDWIKE.

Mr. Frank Peel of Heckmondwike in his 'Nonconformity in Spen Valley,' says :—" He was an occasional member of the congregation, and, if he had lived, would doubtless have stood high on the roll of our national poets. As he died when only 19, his life was all too short for great achievements ; but one of his poems, ' Lines written in the Churchyard of Richmond, Yorks.,' is to be found in all the best col- lections of our standard authors. The thin, pale, shrinking lad, who is remembered as being brought by the hand by his bluff uncle Lionel, would doubtless attract little notice, but he possessed rare talents. His father and mother died when he was young, and he and his brother lived with their aunt, Mrs. Phillips, of Pollard Hall, Gomersal. He was educated, in early life at a school taught by Mr. Horsfall in the village, where, his great talents becoming manifest, he was sent to Richmond Grammar School. Whilst there he evinced poetic ability of no mean order, and forwarded one of his productions to Southey, asking leave to dedicate it to him.   He is buried in the Chapelyard at Heckmondwike.   The inscription on his tombstone is as follows :—

HERBERT KNOWLES,

Died February 17th, 1817.

His superior genius engaged for him the patronage of men eminent for rank, talents, and learning, but the ardour of his mind destroyed the mortal tenement, and he fell a victim to consumption at the age of 19 years."

In attempting to gain any idea of the personality of the young poet we are heavily handicapped.   He was, I believe, dark complexioned, almost certainly pale and delicate looking, judging from his studious habits and his own description of his feeble constitution. There is some evidence of a great shock or sorrow in his life, probably of a romantic nature.   If the two poems of his which have appeared be contrasted, an immense change in sentiment and expression will be observed.   The one entitled ' People will Talk,' is simply the work of a clever and precocious lad, with some powers of observation and neatness in stringing rhymes together; the other is poetry, and poetry of a very elevated kind.   Beyond a certain sense of order I cannot discover the remotest internal evidence to show that the poems are by the same hand, and the advance is so great that it would seem to be due to some more quickening influence than the addition of a year or two of ordinary experience.   More satisfactory, though still vague, evidence is to be found in his letter to Southey.   The expression 'cares and sorrows peculiarly my own,' might be supposed to refer to his dis- like of the prospect of a mercantile career, but when supplemented by ' the little inward peace which the wreck of passion has left behind,' another significance may not unreasonably be attached to it.

Another correspondent sends us a biographical notice very similar to the above, together with the lines on ' The Three Tabernacles,' and the following additional example of the poet's writings, viz.: ' People will Talk.'   Very high praise can be given to the poet's diction, at least in ' The Three Tabernacles ' and the letter to Southey.   In the former it is so weighted with meaning as hardly to be noticed—perhaps the highest praise that can be given.   In the latter it has, in a certain studied deliberation, a great flavour of Dr. Johnson's epistolary style.   It may be interesting to the curious to remember one or two outside events which are always useful in enabling one to understand a period.   During the early years of the century, the Napoleonic wars were raging in different parts of the continent (in 1815, when Herbert Knowles was in his 18th year, the battle of Waterloo was fought), and no doubt the account of those stirring struggles would have a strong effect upon a vivid imagination. Nearer home, in 1812, the Luddite riots filled this part of the country with apprehension, and though it is not unlikely that Knowles might be at Canterbury then, he would hear much about the rising from his relatives. The readers of 'Shirley' will note that when at Pollard Hall he must have been within a minute's walk of Briarmains, the residence of Mr. Yorke. The period was rich in poetical literature. Sir Walter Scott, Byron, Shelley, Keats, Wordsworth, Coleridge, and Southey, all being actively engaged at the same time, while the fiction was of a romantic and often supernatural character, Sir Walter Scott and Sam Radcliffe being the most popular writers in that department. No representative of this branch of the Knowles' family now resides at Gomersal, and their property has passed into other hands. See Cudworth's 'Round about Bradford,' pp. 522-3. &c. Often as the 'Lines written in Richmond Churchyard' • have been printed, a Guide to Richmond might well be deemed defective, which omitted to repeat them. They are from the pen of an amiable and highly gifted youth, who was cut off at the early age of nineteen, whilst preparing, under the kind and assiduous tutelage of Mr. Tate, to enter on his studies at Cambridge. His friends, who were respectable manufacturers at Gomersal, near Leeds, had endeavoured to fix his mind to business, and it was not until he had run off and enlisted in the Artillery, that they consented to allow him to follow the bent of his aspiring genius. He had already attracted the notice of Mr. Southey, and high indeed were the anticipations of his future eminence, but a few short weeks of disease hurried him off to the grave, where the 'device' of the poet, and the 'knowledge' of the scholar are alike strangers. Little was wanting, under God, to his well-being, both at school and at the university, but health. The lamp was consumed by the fire which burned in it. See 'Notes and Queries,' 2nd series, vol. viii., pp. 28, 55, 79, 116, 153; vol. ix., p. 94. &c.; also Robinson's 'Guide to Richmond,' 1833, pp. 60-63. &c.

In the churchyard at Richmond may be observed the tomb of Christopher Clarkson, Esq., F.S.A., the author of a 'History of Richmond,' who died in 1833. This churchyard will also possess to many tourists a touching interest from its associations with Herbert Knowles. This gifted young poet, whose first effort Southey regarded as 'brimful of power and promise,' died in 1817, at the early age of nineteen. His 'Lines written in the Churchyard at Richmond,' beginning

"Methinks it is good to be here."

are well-known. See 'Gentleman's Magazine' for 1819, vol. lxxxix.

pp. 255-6; Chambers's 'Cyclopædia of Literature,' vol. ii., p. 411 ; Smith's 'Old Yorkshire,' vol. iii., pp. 210-11, by the late S. Rayner, of Pudsey; Taylor's 'Worthies of Leeds,' &c., pp. 266-7; and for an account of Charles James Knowles, Esq., Q.C., his brother, see ' Supplement to Leeds Worthies,' pp. 633-4, &c.

[The Editor of this work contributed a notice of Herbert Knowles to the *Cleckheaton Guardian* in May last year, which was replied to by "Junius, Gomersal." The compiler of this sketch has woven the two accounts together, with other original information.]

The Three Tabernacles.

Written in the Churchyard at Richmond, Yorkshire.

'' It is good for us to be here; if thou wilt let us make here three tabernacles, one for Thee, one for Moses, and one for Elias. ''

MATT. XVII. C. 4.

METHINKS it is good to be here,
If thou wilt, let us build; but for whom ?
Nor Elias nor Moses appear,
But the shadows of eve that encompass the gloom,
The abode of the dead, and the place of the tomb.

Shall we build to Ambition ? Oh, no!
Affrighted he shrinketh away :
For, see, they would pin him below
In a small narrow cave, and begirt with cold clay,
To the meanest of reptiles a peer and a prey.

To Beauty ? Ah, no ! she forgets
The charms which she wielded before,
Nor knows the foul worm that she frets,
The skin which but yesterday fools could adore
For the smoothness it held, or the tint which it wore.

Shall we build to the purple of Pride ?
The trappings which dizen the proud ?
Alas ! they are all laid aside ;
And here's neither dress nor adornment allowed,
But the long winding-sheet, and the fringe of the shroud.

To Riches? Alas! 'tis in vain,
Who hid, in their turns have been hid:
The treasures are squandered again,
And here, in the grave are all metals forbid,
But the tinsel that shone on the dark coffin-lid.

To the pleasures which Mirth can afford?
The revel, the laugh, and the jeer?
Ah! here is a plentiful board,
But the guests are all mute as their pitiful cheer,
And none but the worm is a reveller here.

Shall we build to Affection and Love?
Ah no! they have withered and died,
Or fled with the spirit above.
Friends, brothers, and sisters are laid side by side,
Yet none have saluted, and none have replied.

Unto Sorrow? The dead cannot grieve,
Not a sob nor a sigh meet mine ear,
Which compassion itself could relieve!
Ah, sweetly they slumber, nor hope, love, nor fear;
Peace, peace, is the watchword, the only one here.

Unto Death, to whom monarchs must bow?
Ah, no! for his empire is known,
And here there are trophies enow;
Beneath the cold dead, and around the dark stone,
Are the sign of a sceptre that none may disown.

The first tabernacle to HOPE we will build,
And look for the sleepers around us to rise!
The second to FAITH, which ensures it fulfill'd;
And the third to the LAMB of the great sacrifice,
Who bequeathed us them both when he rose to the skies.

People Will Talk.

You may get through the world, but 'twill be very slow,
If you listen to all that is said as you go
You'll be worried, and fretted, and kept in a stew;
For meddlesome tongues must have something to do—
And people will talk.

If quite and modest, you'll have it presumed
That your humble position is only assumed,
You're a wolf in sheep's clothing, or else you're a fool ;
But don't get excited, keep perfectly cool—
    For people will talk.

And then, if you show the least boldness of heart,
Or a slight inclination to take your own part,
They will call you an upstart, conceited, and vain ;
But keep straight ahead, don't stop to explain—
    For people will talk.

If threadbare your dress, and old-fashioned your hat,
Someone will surely take notice of that,
And hint rather strong that you can't pay your way ;
But don't get excited, whatever they say—
    For people will talk.

If your dress is in fashion, don't think to escape,
For they criticise then in a different shape-—
You're ahead of your means, or you're tailor's unpaid ;
But mind your own business, there's nought to be made—
    For people will talk.

Now the best way to do is to do as you please,
For your mind, if you have one, will then be at ease,
Of course you will meet with all sorts of abuse ;
But don't think to stop them—it ain't any use—
    For people will talk.

Forgiveness.

FORGIVE thy foes ! nor that alone,
    Their evil deeds with good repay ;
Fill those with joy who leave thee none,
    And kiss the hand upraised to slay.

So does the fragrant sandal bow,
    In meek forgiveness to its doom,
And o'er the axe at every blow
    Sheds in abundance rich perfume.

JOHN   HUTCHINSON   KNOWLES.

BY THE REV. THOMAS KING, M.A.

VICAR OF HARTSHEAD.

JOHN HUTCHINSON KNOWLES was born at Robertown, in the parish
of Liversedge, on the 19th February, 1827. His father, Mr. George
Knowles, was a schoolmaster in the village, having opened the
" Hall Domain School" in 1817, which he carried on as a boarding
and day school. Mr. Knowles, senior, afterwards removed to Hightown. Here, young Knowles passed his early manhood, first as a
wire-worker, then in a worsted warehouse, and occasionally assisted
his father in the school.

In 1865 he was appointed Clerk to the Cleckheaton Co-operative
Society, which position he still holds. Having earned and deserved the
confidence of his fellow-townsmen, they elected him ten years ago a
member of the Cleckheaton Local Board. His shrewd common sense
and business qualities were soon appreciated by his colleagues on the
Board, who have twice placed him in the important position of Chairman of the Board. He is also one of the Vice-Presidents of the
Cleckheaton Chamber of Commerce.

In his earnest desire to help his fellow-men, spiritually as well as
temporally, he some years ago occasionally occupied the pulpit as a
local preacher among the Free Methodists, but was obliged to relin-
quish that work owing to the continually increasing labour and responsibility of his daily calling. He has been a total abstainer for 35 years
and has been in the van of the temperance movement as an ardent
advocate.

Of the many parts which he has so ably played in life, music and
poetry have had their share. Very early in life he exhibited a passion
for music—vocal and instrumental—which is shown in his skilful play-
ing of the violin, violoncella and double-bass. As a singer his fine
mellow-bass voice has given pleasure to all who have heard it. For
nearly thirty years he has been a prominent member of the Cleckheaton
Philharmonic Society, and is now doing good service as their double-
bass player. As a teacher of music he has been very successful, and

I am, yours truly
J H Knowles

as a musical composer of anthems, songs, psalms, and hymn tunes, he has attained some celebrity. The father's musical gift has passed unto his children, as he has quite a musical family.

His poetic ability has found vent in the composition of various poems which have appeared from time to time in the poet's corner of the local papers. We are not aware that his poems have been collected and published in a volume, but we would give expression to the hope that Mr. Knowles may some day give to the world the productions of his poet's genius. Mr. Knowles is a genial and an openhearted fellow, and highly respected by all who have the pleasure of his acquaintance.

Hartshead Church.

A Meditation.

ANCIENT edifice ! venerable pile !
What thoughts arise as on thy rugged walls
We stand and gaze ! Historic centuries
Have co-existed with thy chequered course,
And could thy walls receive vocality,
What revelations of the lives and deeds
Of high and low of generations past
We then should have presented to our view !
Monarchs have appeared and have departed,
And left their records to posterity ;
And trusted ministers and parliaments
Have had their day, and likewise disappear'd ;
The people, too, have struggled and have toil'd
Progressively throughout the centuries
Of misty ignorance, despair and hope,
Right down to this our blest Victorian age,
And having oft their rightful claims declar'd
Have now become a power in the state.
These many changeful times thou hast surviv'd
And unpretentiously thy lot sustained.

Of elevation high, thou art in truth
A landmark 'mongst the many hills around.
From off thy tower what rare expanse of view !
Here may be observed the mountains eastward

Bearing towards the German Ocean ; southward
Are the bounding hills of counties Derby
And of Nottingham ; then looking westward,
Is the noted 'backbone of old England ; '
And northward is discerned, out-stretching far
In native garb, bold, pleasing Rombalds Moor.
Within thine inner range secluded stands
'Mid stately trees and tinted foliage
The old Baronial home of Armytage,—
The long-renown'd and far-fam'd Kirklees Hall.
Hard by is seen the quaint and weird remains
Of Kirklees' ancient nunnery, and where
' Bold Robin Hood' met with his tragic death.
How alter'd is the scene ! these hill and vales
Which, times long past, were oft the rendezvous
Of the free-booter and his ' merrie men,'
Now speak to us in times more civilized.
Here husbandry in vastly better forms
Is now in operation ; and commerce
In all its many phases and degrees
Is well develop'd ; and industrial hives
Now thickly stud the area around :
Yes, through all this, old Kirk, thou hast remain'd,
And hast thy functions quietly fulfilled.

God's house ! His temple ! His dispensary !
Where He has frequently bestowed His gifts
To way-worn, seeking, and receiving souls.
Here hath the words of life oft been proclaimed
By faithful messengers, and in the roll
A Ryley, Ismay, Harrison, and Wood,
A Hall, a Lucas, and a Roberson,
A Brontë, and an Atkinson. a Webb,
And now, in continuity, a King.*

Thy three old bells have oft-times spoken out
Of local and of national events,
And told of each returning Sabbath day :
But, sad to know, two long have voiceless been,
And have had to rest in sullen silence
To listen to the oft-repeated clang
Of their loquacious but enfeebled mate.†

* The Rev. Thomas King, M.A., who is the present vicar.
† A couplet runs : ' " There's the old church of Hartshead-cum-Clifton,
' Where are two crack'd bells and a snip'd 'un."

HARTSHEAD CHURCH.

Although impaired, yet oh, how changeable
That solitary voice within thy tower
Has frequently become!   The loving pair
On matrimony bent, have joyfully
Embraced its *special* invitation, 'Come!'
And then have each to each their troth declared.
The weary toiler, on each holy day
Has listened to the *welcome* voice, 'Come, come!'
Then with the worshippers has praised his God,
Received the Word, and found his strength renewed.
But, to the funereal retinue
A *solemn* 'Come, come, come,' that bell has toll'd;
And thus have mourners, sad and weeping, laid
Aside their loved ones in the silent grave.

Around thee rest, in quietness and peace,
The mouldered and the mouldering dust of hosts
Who once did live this mortal life of ours,—
Yes, hosts on hosts of them, both small and great!
And here I may ('tis weakness or 'tis not)
Recall fond memories of those who loved
And cared for me, through childhood and through youth:
A tender father and a mother dear;
And others of my kin, there, there, *they* rest;
And with the host surrounding, now await
The trumpet-call of resurrection morn.
What is the lesson?   All the dead have lived,
And all who live, and shall live, too must die,—
'Tis God's appointment this with mortal man.
But if man dies, shall he not live again?
Yes, yes; within thy sacred, hallow'd walls,
God's great compassion to a fallen world,
And, in return, man's duty towards his God,
Are ever and anon in love proclaimed.
Thus man may live in peace with God on earth,
And then eternally with God in heaven.

Ancient edifice! venerable pile!
Again we gaze upon thy rugged walls,
Thy walls which, more than seven centuries
Have stood in honour'd form, as now they do,
And as we gaze, may we express the hope
That God, in His abounding providence,

May still regard thee with His special care;
As time reveals His coming years
  Of sunshine and of storm,
May He preserve with tenderness
  Thy ancient, weather'd form,
That hosts of our race who on earth yet shall live,
May honour thee, and may God's blessing receive.

Ode on Christmas.

Hail, sacred day! great Christmas day, all hail!
Time's revolutions speaks thee here again,
And we to thee a hearty welcome give.
What fond renewals of sweet friendship, greet
This sacred and auspicious day! what joy
Is realized when pilgrim-parents meet
Again around the welcome, festive board,
In health and peace, their earthly heritage!
What fond embraces, counsels, pledges, joys!
And then what tears when call'd another time
To part, it may be—the last time on earth.

What old and social friendships are renewed!
What touching mem'ries crowd upon the mind
When friend meets friend! though often marr'd by thoughts
Of some who once appeared as well as they,
But who, since last they met, have died and left
The world! alas how many we once call'd
Our friends, are now amongst the silent dead!

And who in friendship's circle shall survive
Another revolution of old time?
We must not, cannot tell.   But why despond?
On this great day a Saviour was revealed,—
The one in Bethlehem born.—Great Prince of Peace,
Man's great Atoner and Restorer too:
(Time's most rejoiceful, mem'rable event)

1

Yes He, the gift of Heaven—on this day born,—
Became our one great Sacrifice : and now
By His vicarious death upon the cross, ·
We each may live, and die, and get to heaven.

If so, then why bewail our lot on earth ?
And why lament the alternating scenes
Of good old Christmas ?   Let us but improve
The time allotted us for life and death,
By best endeavours to live Christ-like both
With God and man.   Thus shall we realize
In God's good time an entrance into bliss
Abundant ; and where all may sweetly spend
Ecstatic and eternal holy-day.
There all may meet, and·heav'ns' sweet pleasures share,
And death and partings shall be no more known.

Psalm I.

THE man is blest who never treads
   The path of wicked men ;
Who never seeks to gain a seat
   Within the scorner's den.

But whose delight is with the Lord,
   And in His holy law ;
Who daily meditates therein,
   His Father's will to know.

Like as a tree whose roots are found
   By river's water pure :
Fruit he shall bear ;—and with his deeds
   Prosperity is sure.

Not so with base, ungodly men,
   On sin and scorning bent ;
In God's just judgment they shall meet
   Their self-wrought punishment.

God knows the righteous ; and for them
   He has rewards in store ;
Whilst they whose ways are wickedness
   Shall perish evermore.

THOMAS NAYLOR.

By P. H. DAVIS, Ph.D. F.R.G.S.

EDITOR OF "THE SMOKER"; MEMBER OF THE SOCIETY OF CHEMICAL
INDUSTRY; MEMBER OF THE SOCIETY OF ARTS; FELLOW
OF THE ROYAL HISTORICAL SOCIETY, ETC., ETC.

THOMAS NAYLOR was born on the 2nd day of February, 1828, at
Cleckheaton, and received his early education at the hands of Mr.
Anderton who every Sunday held a bible class. He afterwards attended
the schools in connection with St. John's in his native town. He was
brought up as a shoemaker, a vocation which he still follows. He
became an Oddfellow early in life, and obtained the dignity of Past
District Grand Master. He was also instrumental in promoting the
Cleckheaton Conservative Club, and was an active member for a great
number of years, being held in high esteem by the members. Their
confidence in him and appreciation of his services took a practical
shape on April 16th, 1883, when he was publicly presented with his
life-sized portrait in oils.

Mr. Naylor has ever been ready with voice and pen to support the
Conservative cause, and on one occasion he was specially selected to
speak at London in support of Viscount Cranbrook's motion of confidence in Lord Derby's Government.

His poems have appeared in *The Yorkshire Post, The Cleckheaton
Guardian,* and *The Cleckheaton Advertiser.*

Lines on the Death of the late Lord Beaconsfield.

BRITONS mourn! your noble senator's no more,
His brilliant fame has spread from shore to shore;
For the British Isles he's laboured hard and long,
But now he's gone to join the celestial throng.

L 2

What powers to lead, and what a noble mind!
The nation feels the gap he's left behind;
In our day his like will ne'er be seen,
He was so loyal to his country and Queen.

Though from the ranks and friendless, still he rose
And became the leader in a noble cause,
He persevered with what he took in hand,
And beneath his banner rallied a gallant band.

Our senator now has left the field of fame,
Where for himself he gained a glorious name;
For British interests to him were ever dear,
And when duty called he never knew a fear.

Twice at the helm he steered the royal ship,—
His works will follow but a nation's left to weep;
At the Berlin Congress the despot heaved a sigh,
For " Peace with honour " was our gallant chieftain's cry.

In Europe, too, his praise is loudly sung,
By every nation and by almost every tongue;
They mourn the loss that Britain will sustain,
To the nations around us our loss will be no gain.

What footprints now our chieftain's left behind,
What brilliant thoughts from an ever active mind;
His name in history will be handed down
As a statesman and orator of great renown.

What man can lay his hand upon his heart
And say our chief has not played well his part?
Britain's honour he was always proud to guard,
And a generous nation gave him his reward.

In Hughenden church-yard our chieftain chose
Where his remains might rest in sweet repose;
No pomp, no vanity, nor unnecessary strife,
But they calmly laid him with his late partner in life.

Sleep on, late senator, in thy eternal rest,
Though absent from us, thy spirit's with the blest;
Britons fain their homage would have paid,
And thy remains in our ancient abbey laid.

MARK J. NELSON.

BY JOSEPH GAUNT, B.A. B.Sc.

AUTHOR OF "EVENTIDE," "MARAH'S REVENGE," ETC.; VICE-
PRESIDENT YORKSHIRE LITERARY SOCIETY.

IN 1858 S. Clegg & Co., of Heckmondwike, printed a 16 pp.
pamphlet entitled "Poetic Lines: composed and written by an invalid,
on his bed of affliction." I have discovered that the invalid, was
Mark J. Nelson, who formerly resided at Wyke Lane, Wyke, but
beyond this I have been unable to obtain any further information of
Mr. Nelson. The little work contains thirteen poems and a lengthy
preface. From this latter we learn that the poems were composed "to
beguile a tedious hour while confined to my bed "—"that it is the
first attempt of anything of the kind; and in all human probability it
will be the last. But I trust the reader, whoever he may be, will be
kind enough to take the dross along with the ore, as there must
necessarily be many errors, written by one who could never parse a
sentence or conjugate a verb."

All for the Best.

OH! home of my childhood, fain would I view thee,
   And walk once again o'er thy green fields so fair ;
But alas! I do fear I'm where I must still be,
   Till removed I am from all pain and care
By the hand that is o'er me, as 'twere in danger
   As though to correct me, a sinner confessed,
And keep me by this from a far greater danger,
   Then let me not murmur for God knows the best.
Oh! where are the friends with whom I did wander ?
   Some gone to their rest, others healthy and free,
While I'm here secluded from scenes that are grander,
   And left to bewail fate's eternal decree ;
No, I'll not murmur, what the use of complaint,
   As though I was the first that e'er was distress'd,
Still will I hope it is but a wise training,
   And all will be well, for God knows the best ;

Then let us hope the Lord won't despise us,
    If we only bend to his merciful yoke;
But leave all behind who fain would advise us
  ·To live on in sin, His wrath to invoke.

The Church-going Bell.

How oft have I stood to hear the bell tolling,
    To summon the peasantry clad in their best,
As well as the gentry in vehicles rolling,
    To honour the day set apart for our rest:
And each have a chance of there unfolding
    All sin and impurity from their own breast,
When they all would confess how they'd gone astray,
And like sheep lacking shepherd had lost the true way.

How well did it sound to hear them confessing,
    Their sin and their shame in the House of the Lord,
For so to unburden indeed 'tis a blessing,
    That few things on earth such pleasures afford;
Moreover the pastor was kindly addressing,
    His hearers to foster both peace and concord,
And show to the world how Christians live,
And so induce others it a trial to give.

Sonnet, on September.

THE Summer's sultry heat is waining fast,
    And rich September in her plent'ous train
Does bring for man, which she before him casts,
    Prolific store of fruit, of root and grain;
Be not ungrateful then, O man, but praise
    The giver of all good, to thee and thine;
Yea, to him a tribute of thanksgiving raise,
    Nor e'er worship at a less worthy shrine.
A thankful heart does most contentment bring;
    I like not much the supplicating mood,
But raise by voice in songs divine, to sing
    The praise of Him, the author of all good;
To bear with resignation earthly care,
And spurn from me the monster, grim despair.

MRS. J. S. NORTH.

By JOHN FIRTH.

EDITOR "CLECKHEATON GUARDIAN,"

MRS. NORTH *nee* Julia A. Hey, is the only daughter of Mr. J. G. Hey, of Brookhouse, Hartshead Moor, Cleckheaton. She was born at Hightown, Liversedge, September 19th, 1849, and was educated, in the first place at Mrs. Mitchell's seminary, Cleckheaton, and sub-sequently at the Moravian Ladies' School, Gomersal. The latter she left when about seventeen years of age. Her parents removed to Brookhouse in 1858, and being an only child, and of delicate constitu-tion, she has remained with them ever since her marriage. In early life Miss Hey displayed traces of deep religious thought, and a love of nature—full of feeling and sympathy for the suffering. As she grew in years her religious convictions deepened, and she felt a desire to devote her life to a noble object in the service of God, but her brave resolves were to some extent frustrated owing to her earthly tenement being of the frailest description. She however resolved to do all that her physical powers would permit of. A favourable opportunity offered itself in the erection of the Broomfield United Methodist Free Church Chapel, soon after leaving school, which chapel was contiguous to her home. Here she was prevailed upon to take charge of the young women's select class, and she soon gathered round her, numerous young people who through her example and precept became co-workers in God's vineyard. In connection with the good work carried on at this chapel Miss Hey was foremost in every movement, whether it was the Band of Hope, the Mutual Improvement Classes, the working parties for bazaar purposes, or the choir. One of her most happy efforts deserves special attention. It was a Saturday evening class for young women, in connection with which needlework, dress-cutting, cooking, and other household duties were taught, much no doubt to the well-being of the members of the class. Indeed it may be said in a word that Miss Hey was a willing helper in all the Christian and philanthropic work of the district. In 1887 she married Mr. John S. North, a fellow-worker in Church and Sunday School work. It is a matter however of general regret to her friends that Mrs. North is so

often laid aside, for weeks and months at a time, as at present, suffering
most acutely from a severe affliction of the heart, and chronic asthma.
It is almost needless to add that she bears her suffering with patience
and Christian fortitude.   Of Mrs. North's ability as a poet it is
preferred to leave the readers to judge for themselves, after saying that
some of her poems give evidence of considerable merit.   She has now
in the press a little work, to be called " Poems and Essays."

Our Picnic.

" ONCE upon a time " as writers oft say,
A party set out, very soon in the day,
　For the famous time-worn Bolton Abbey ;
From Brighouse and neighbourhood, most of them hail'd,
And to catch the train none of them failed,
　Though none had the aid of a cabby.

The morning certainly was rather dull,
But all the party of fun were so full
　They feared not the state of the weather ;
So from Bradford they rode in carriages—first class—
(Put in by the Guard, who'd an eye to a glass,)
　With hearts gay and light as a feather.

Having breakfasted early, before leaving home,
They wished for a second, ere they further did roam
　On their journey of innocent pleasure ;
So in Ilkley they gazed, with hungry haste,
And espied very soon a place to their taste,
　Where they could sit and eat at their leisure.

They then hired a carriage, two horses, a man,
And then with their tricks they once more began,
　As they journey'd 'long Addingham Road.
They laughed, and they talked, though none of them sang,
But they had scraps of poetry, from one—Mr. Lang—
　And none seemed to bear sorrow's load.

There were Wilkinson's, Farrar's, and that not a few,
Holmes, Shackleton, Lang, and Walker, Hey—no !
　Altogether they numbered thirteen.
Sometimes races were run, and flowers were plucked,
And some were so dusty, in the Wharfe they were ducked,
　And " lang " after in their hats were seen.

They journeyed along past the " Devonshire Arms "
And reached the Abbey, where they now sang psalms,
  And they gazed on those ruins so old—
Those mighty relics of bygone days,
Giving us an idea of monastic ways,
  And of myst'ries no tongue can unfold.

To the stepping stones, firm in the river's bed,
They next wended their way, though with dizzy head,
  Some crossed o'er the bright sparkling river.
Their cry " Onwards, upwards, to the top of the hill,"
Where with rapturous delight, they all stood still
  And gazed at the ruins and river.

They retraced their steps now over the stones,
Cross'd without accident, or audible moans,
  The strong kindly helping the weak.
And now came the great event of the day—
Their photos were taken without much delay,
  For the man was not far to seek.

To arrange each person to their liking and will,
Took a little time, and required some skill,
  But yet in the bud it was done,—
Just imagine the group, some sitting, some stood,
Each trying their best to look very good,
  Yet all the time brimful of fun.

This business concluded, they drove to the Strid,
Where anyone quickly of life may be rid,
  So great is the rush and the roar.
They lingered not long, but ascended with speed
The hill to the cottage, for they dinner did need,
  For hunger now tempted them sore.

Being refreshed by dinner, a wash, and a rest,
They to Barden Tower now thought it best
  To walk, that they the ruins might see.
The clouds now gathered, the rain did descend,
As back to the Strid they their footsteps did wend,
  The rain rather damping their glee.

On entering the carriage, their spirits revived,
Though it rained so hard, they might almost have dived
  In the stream on the waterproof (?) cover.
They in each others faces the water did throw,
So all were baptized by sprinkling now,
  Nay, some were wet nearly all over.

And now, how delightful the party all looked,   ·
With feathers uncurled, and umbrellas all soaked,
    And the starch from their linen washed out.
Poor half-drown'd creatures, they looked such a sight,
'Twas a pity to see them in such a sad plight,
    But they enjoyed themselves there was no doubt.

Arriving at Ilkley at five thirty-five,
And partaking of tea to keep spirits alive,
    They prepared to start home by the train ;
So to Bradford they went, in carriage—third class—
For no guard now appeared, so they went with the mass
    Of people sent home by the rain.

They arrived at the "Midland" at Bradford, too late,
Yet on their way to the "L.Y." their speed ne'er did 'bate,
    But arriving, the first train had gone.
So some had to wait, but with "good nights" sincere,
They parted, and went to the homes held most dear,
    And so ended their long day of fun.

To a White Chrysanthemum.

THANKS to the fair hand that gathered thee—
Emblem of spotless purity—
Pure are thy numberless petals of white,
Silently speaking of the Land of Light ;
Thou'rt come to brighten the sick-room's shade,
Come to give hope, though earth's hopes are delayed,
And these are the words, methinks I hear :
"We flowers may fade, but thou need'st not fear,
They shall stand forever, the Words of the Lord,
And His promises too, are as sure as His word."

Thoughts after a Service.

How glorious here to meet and praise
    Our God and Heavenly King,
To read His word, speak of his love
    And hallelujahs sing.

Tho' when we meet together here,
 Time calls us soon away;
But when we reach that Heavenly shore
 It will be perfect day.

Time may roll on upon this earth,
 And flowers bloom and die;
Winter may come and summer warm,
 And autumn winds may sigh.

Spring too may come with its bright flowers,
 But all will soon decay;
But in that bright celestial land,
 Time ne'er shall pass away.

'Twill be one long eternal day
 And there shall be no night,
Nothing but joy, and love, and peace,
 And angels faces bright.

Dead and Gone.

DEAD!—Why say she's dead?
She has but laid her tired head
In the arms of sleep, death's quiet sleep
From which, tho' she slumber long and deep
 Her body shall be raised.

Gone!—yes gone—and where?
Far—oh far away from here—
Her spirit's fled—like many more
Has now reached the eternal shore
 Where sorrows never come.

Blest soul!—her trials o'er—
Sorrows will be felt no more
Her body will be no more racked
With pain, nor sin can e'er distract
 Her thoughts from God again.

In Memoriam.

WALKER GREEN, AGED 13 YEARS.

(A Scholar in Broomfield Sunday School, who was killed at Flatts Pit,
June 8th, 1885.)

WITH strange bewildering suddenness,
　God's warning voice comes to our school;
We hear the call with solemn awe,
　And feelings we can scarce control.

Life's slender thread, how quickly cut!
　No eye beholding his sad fall
But God's—who's eyes can pierce the earth,
　And watches o'er us, one and all.

Father, Thou knowest what is best,
　We ask for grace to bear Thy will;
Speak to the parents' troubled hearts,
　And whisper softly, " Peace, be still."

There is a land, no danger there,
　No parting, and no falling tear:
No sudden death, no mourning class,
　No saddened heart, no funeral bier.

Oh! may we for the end prepare,
　Which comes alike to young and old;
May we prepare to meet Him, where
　The brightest glories will unfold.

'Choose ye whom ye will Serve.'

OH! choose ye whom you'll serve this day:
Yourselves, decked out in raiments gay?
Or gold, or jewels, or silver bright?
Or revel in the haunts of night?

But choose ye whom you'll serve just now,
And in true grace and knowledge grow,
And live to serve your God aright,
·Then dwell in realms of love and light.

Oh that all men would choose the King
Of Heaven, then all the earth would ring
With loud hosannas; then the Lord
Would give to each his bright reward.

Our Future.

OUR future lies in shadow,
    Its joys we may not see :
We cannot read its pages,
    Or know what " is to be.
Yet onward, step by step, we tread,
Sometimes in hope, sometimes in dread :
    Hope with its golden sunlight,
        E'er bids us " trust and live,"
    For brighter days are waiting
        Their joy and peace to give.
It bids us smile, be brave and strong,
And wend our way with a psalm and song.

Our future lies in shadow,
    Its shadows are not known :
We may not feel its anguish,
    Or know whom we may mourn ;
But gentle and loving is the hand
That leads through earth to our Father's land.
    That Hand will soothe our suffering,
        And point to rest above :
    Will help us bear our burdens
        With tender, patient love ;
Will give us faith to be brave and strong,
Though our days of pain be sad and long.

The Lord will be a Refuge in Time of Trouble.

I KNOW that I am weak
And unworthy to speak
To God, our Maker and Lord,
But His Son came to save
Us from sin and the grave,
So I venture my all on His word.

'Tis not always bright,
Very oft the sun's light
Is hid by thick clouds from our gaze ;
We must trust in our Guide,
And keep close to His side,
Thro' the sunshine and storms of our days.

He will give us His grace
To meet face to face
Th' afflictions and trials that rise ;
And at last we shall hear
His voice, and shall wear
Our crown in our home in the skies.

My Wish to be like Jesus.

I WANT to be like Jesus, so holy, kind, and true,
I want to be like Jesus, and all things gentle do ;
I want to be like Jesus in every word and deed,
I want to be like Jesus, sowing heavenly seed.

I want to be like Jesus, and sinning mortals seek,
And tell them of that Jesus, forgiving, pure, and meek ;
I want to be like Jesus, each straying lamb to feed,
And be to them like Jesus, a friend in pain and need.

Then when I'm called by Jesus to leave this world of care
I'll go to dwell with Jesus, and be for ever there ;
I'll sing the praise of Jesus, and play that harp of gold,
And see the face of Jesus, who's love can ne'er be told.

CHARLOTTE OATES.

BY BUTLER WOOD.

CHIEF LIBRARIAN, BRADFORD FREE LIBRARY, ETC.

——

THE subject of this sketch, Miss Charlotte Oates, was born at Halifax on the 27th of April, 1856. When she was quite young her parents went to live at Daisy Cottage, near Wyke, and there a comfortable *partie carsé*, the family of four still reside. Although the locality, Horse Close, is not very far from the foundries of the Low Moor Company, it is nevertheless both out of sight and sound of the iron-works. From her dwelling place, instead of the smoke of the furnaces may be seen glorious woodlands, and even the distant moorlands which form the natural barrier between the counties of Lancashire and Yorkshire. In this quite and retired corner the poetic talent inherited from her mother has had ample opportunity of development, indeed it is quite evident from her productions that Miss Oates's poetic gifts have not been suffered to

> " Blush unseen,
> Nor waste their sweetness on the desert air."

At the age of twenty-one she contributed her first poem to the *Blackpool Herald*, and since that time most of the local papers, especially those of the Spen Valley district, have published poems from her pen. She is a genuine and enthusiastic lover of nature in all its moods and variations, and she possesses in a marked degree the faculty of rendering her impressions of it in poetical language.

Her poetry is noticeable for its facile execution, spontaneous flow of ideas; many of which are both striking and original, and for a certain amount of imaginative power. Those entitled " A December Rose," " Moonlit Flowers," and " The Afterglow," are of a distinctly able character, and stamp the writer as a genuine poet. Although many of her poems have been published in various news-papers, more have still to see the light, and it is to be hoped that Miss Oates may at some future time see her way to publish a selection in book form.

Moonlit Flowers.

Moon of the summer night,
Soft and subdued thy light,
Kissing the roses white,
    The while they sleep.

Roses so rich and fair,
Filling the evening air,
While ye are slumb'ring there,
    With perfume sweet.

Softly the summer breeze,
Speaks to the moonlit trees,
Plays with the cream-white leaves,
    Where dewdrops gleam.

Only to look at them!
Trembles each liquid gem,
Poised on the mossy stem,
    So crystal clear.

Down in the fair rose bower,
Drooping its head still lower,
Blushes the sweet-pea flower,
    And clasps the rose.

With clinging tendrils fine,
Lovingly they entwine,
Dew-jewelled flowers of mine,
    This summer night.

After the sunshine warm,
Bathed in their nightly balm,
Wearing a fresher charm,
    Beneath the moon.

Transient gifts from heaven!
Scenting the breath of even;
Would that to each were given
    Perpetual life!

Taking its own sweet will,
Straying along the sill,
Into my chamber, still,
    Peeps one white rose.

Into the shadows deep,
Hither it fain would creep,
Bowing its head in sleep,
    Against the pane.
Rose of a summer's day,
Born but to fade away :
Frailer than mortal clay,
    And lacks the soul.
Whispers this dreaming rose,
Wrapt in its calm repose,
"Time for the eyes to close,
    Good night, good night!"

Retrospection.

WHEN looking back on the bygone years,
The lights and shadows, the smiles and tears,
The joys and sorrows the heart has known,
And precious boons that have been our own :
The soul goes out in a song of praise
For mercies sweet that have blest our days.
There are no roses without a thorn,
And looking back on afflictions borne,
But seems to heighten and make more dear
The pleasant days that were fair and clear :
The rays of joy on the past we see
Like rainbow tints on a storm-lashed sea :
And Faith has shone like a beacon light,
And soothed the spirit through grief's dark night.
Each natal day there's a sweet content
To backward look on a life well-spent :
On work performed and on duties done,
On the good achieved and the honours won.
Kind words and actions from day to day,
Fall sweet as flowers strewn on life's way.
A life well lived is the best enjoyed :
We measure time as it is employed ;
In joy, on gossamer wings 'tis sped,

K

In pain, it passes on wings of lead ;
And this must solace all hearts opprest
" Who labours hardest finds sweetest rest."
The thoughts turn back, and the past appears,
To dearer grow with the lapse of years ;
And youth resembles, so soon 'tis flown,
The tender light of the dappled dawn ;—
The rosy glow of the eastern skies,
That marks the place where the sun will rise,
The transient glow must too soon give way,
Before the glare of life's fleeting day :
And ere 'tis valued, behold ! we trace,
Time's footsteps left on the care-lined face :
And ere we know it, oft-times are there
His gleams of silver amongst the hair.
Thus age creeps on, as the day will glide,
The sun must set at the evening tide ;
So, one by one, do our friends depart,
And links will break that must wrench the heart.
Each plays his part on the world's wide stage,
Some go when young, and some ripe with age.
Those whom in youth we have loved the best,
Have done their parts and have gone to rest :
Oh ! strange it seems it should oft be so, .
The hearts most cherished are first to go ;
The true ones left, be they ere so few,
Whose friendship came like the grateful dew
That falls so fresh on the verdure parched,
They cheered the way as we onward marched.
Let such be prized while our path they cross,
Like grains of gold on a road of dross.
Till we in turn must obey the call ;
And why should ever the grave appall ?
Life's but the passage to higher things,
Before the spirit has found its wings :
And death is but our chrysalis state,
Whence winged we soar to the Glory-gate !
To enter there in our new array,
The perfect light of a fadeless day ;
No eye of mortal can pierce the veil
That hides the Realms where no ills assail :
May each so live that as fresh years come,
We worthier feel of our Father's Home.

Lost.

THE mackerel boats are sailing
  In beauty side by side ;
They leave the bar, and sail afar,
  All with the midnight tide ;
They're steering for the fishing ground,
  Before the break of day ;
The pale soft light of planets bright,
  Illumes their trackless way.

They glide along serenely,
  Beneath the midnight stars ;
The night is warm; no sign of storm
  The placid beauty mars :
No gale distends their russet sails,
  No clouds obscure the sky ;
The sea's at rest, and on its breast,
  No boding shadows lie.

They're anchored now in silence,
  Upon the slumb'ring sea ;
No billow breaks, nor wind awakes,
  'Tis still, as still can be :
No sound is heard among the crews,—
  'Tis like a fleet asleep ;
They throw the bait, and quietly wait,
  Their fortunes on the deep.

  *   *   *   *

The sun arose in splendour,
  Alike on sea and land ;
It threw a ray across the bay,
  And gilded all the strand :
But when it set, it left behind
  A gold and crimson light,
Till like a flame, the sky became,
  Then waned to sable night.

The wind began to murmur,
  In whispers soft and low ;
Then gathered strength, till lo ! at length,
  A gale began to blow :

It wailed around the lonely quay,
    (The smacks had not come home);
No midnight hush, but roll and rush,
    Disturb'd the gathering gloom.

One long unbroken tremour,
    Swelled upward from the deep;
Its dream had broke, its vengeance spoke—
    A giant roused from sleep;
For days the dreadful tempest raged,
    For days the billows tost;
The boats no more came back to shore,
    For all the fleet was lost!

Oh! trusting man, how soon oppressed!
The foam-flecked waters ne'er confessed;
Oh! hapless fleet, oh! tyrant sea,—
Jehovah holds the mystery!

A Wintry Sunset.

How beautiful the sun went down
    Behind yon snow-clad hill;
It tinged the clouds with fiery dye,—
How calm and beautiful they lie—
    And all is sad and still.

Around, above, where e'er I look,
    The scene is one of peace;
The far-off landscape draped in white,
As softly falls the veil of night,
    Its beauties still increase.

The garb of snow brings out in full
    The objects all around;
In bold relief, with tall bare trees
That stand out black, devoid of leaves,
    The distant hills are crowned.

That orb of crimson hue has sunk
    So softly in the west:
Has shed its glory here below,
And kissed the pure crystal snow,
    Before it sunk to rest,

It glimmered brightly through the trees,
And shot a parting ray;
First to the valleys bid good-bye,
Then smiled upon the moorlands high,—
And then it passed away.

Its disc has disappeared from view
And night has cast its pall;
The dappled clouds retain their light,—
Divinely beautiful the sight,—
And peace reigns over all.

A December Rose.

On a solitary rose being found blooming in December on a little girl's grave.

WHEN Winter's hand lay icy cold
Upon the woodlands and the hills,
And in his grasp the streams were locked,
And mute were little wayside rills.

The old graveyard was lone and drear,
Upon that dark December day;
The Frost King touched the withered leaves,
And glittered on the tombstones grey.

I wandered in, I know not why,
In listless mood I love to tread
And meditate, where silence guards
The cheerless precincts of the dead.

I came upon a little grave,
Wherein there lay a sleeping child;
I stood entranced, for there, behold
A lovely rose upon me smiled.

A beauteous red December rose,
Whose perfume filled the frosty air;
It bloomed alone, amidst decay,
For all around was bleak and bare.

It blushed that I had found it dared
In winter time itself reveal;
And through those petals sweet, I felt
The child's own soul to mine appeal.

It bravely bore the biting frost,
  And seemed to me a sacred thing ;
To show that from the deepest gloom
  Of death and winter, life can spring !

An emblem of the child's pure soul,
  And of its love, and faith, and trust ;
The flower it loved in life must needs
  Grow there, above its mortal dust.

'Twas life in death, and seemed to be
  All that a little child would crave,
Whose life was brief, whose death was sweet,
  As that loved flower upon its grave.

A symbol of immortal life—
  The hope that puts to flight all fears ;
The crystal drops stood on that rose ;
  If angels weep, those were their tears.

That precious flower a sign may be,
  Which they have sent to us in love,
To tell us that her spirit now
  Lives fair as it, with them above.

Or is it that the winter rose
  From Paradise was dropt below,
From off her crown, to let us know
  That they have decked that darling's brow ?

To the Sea.

Thunder, thunder, mighty sea,
In thy great sovereignty ;
Speaking as thy billows roll,
Appealing only to the soul.
Always moving, always will,
Restless ocean, never still ; ·
Commanding with imperious voice,
With an awful deafening noise ;
Calling in the solemn gloom,
Hapless victims to their doom.

Soul of fierce despotic power,
Friend and foe in one brief hour!
Man to thee must ever bow:
Many, many moods hast thou;
Beautiful, and weird, and wild—
One day tranquil, calm, and mild,
Shining like a mirror bright,
Rippling in the fair sunlight;
Then as angry thou wilt be,
O thou changing, surging sea!
With thy mighty waves advancing,
And the seething white spray dancing,
In their madden'd fury waking,
Rolling, roaring, bounding, breaking!
With thy broad'ning billows sweeping
Stately forward, booming, leaping;
With thy tossing foam-wreaths dashing,
And thy green-grey colours flashing.
Arch dissembler, too, art thou—
Who would think to see thee now,
Laughing with defiant pride,
That those smiling waters hide
Smould'ring passions laid at rest,
Underneath thy placid breast?
Thou, that only yesterday,
Summoned human lives away:
Many a fond heart was bereft
When thy heaving billows cleft,
Taking at one mighty sweep,
To thy yawning caverns deep,
Those who dared to cope with thee,
O thou grasping, hungry sea!
Challenging, with threat'ning roar,
All who cross from shore to shore.
With thine own mysterious light,
Beautiful thou art to-night;
All is thine that thou canst claim,
And looking on thee we exclaim—
" What wonders in thy waters lurk!
Thou art God's greatest, noblest work."

*Yours Truly
John Eddy*

JOHN ODDY, V.S.

By THE REV. BENJAMIN MAYOU, M.A.

LATE VICAR OF BADDESLEY-ENSOR.

HAVING been called upon to occasionally take services at the Old White Chapel, Cleckheaton, I happened to become somewhat intimately acquainted with Mr. John Oddy, the subject of the present brief memoir. He was born at Tong, near Leeds, on October 4th, 1829. He was brought up with his father and grandfather, and attended the village school until eleven years of age, when he was taught by Mr. William Crowther, of Bramley, for three years. His father and grandfather had all their lives followed the occupation of smiths and farriers, and John decided to adopt that business as a livelihood. With his relatives he remained until twenty-four years of age. In February, 1854, he commenced the practise of Veterinary Surgeon at Cleckheaton, a profession he still follows. He has been on the list of qualified Veterinary Surgeons since the passing of the Act of Parliament about a dozen years ago. He was married to Miss Butler, of Cleckheaton on September 16th, 1857. Ever since he migrated from Tong to Cleckheaton, Mr. Oddy has taken an active interest in Mutual Improvement and other Societies, holding various offices. During a long and eventful life he has also evinced a deep interest in things musical, and played the violoncello at Tong Church; in fact he was choirmaster there for ten years. Mr. Oddy is a life member of the Yorkshire Association of Change Ringers, the Cleckheaton Philharmonic Society, and several other institutions.

The writer has frequently held long conversations with him on medical and other subjects, and always found him well up to date in general knowledge—and many a pleasant chat has he had with him whilst on the way to church—for Mr. Oddy is an ardent Conservative and a true Churchman.

As regards his powers of versification, much might be said; that he is a versatile writer, I think all will admit. His poetry though never reaching a lofty standard, is not by far so servile as much that has been handed down to posterity in volume form. The pieces I have selected viz:—" My Old Anvil Block," " Music," " The Last Hawthorn in Whitcliffe Lane," "Lines on Love," and " Cleckheaton Town Hall Clock and Chimes," will give an accurate description of his style, and will not, I think, be unwelcome to the readers of this volume. Many of Mr. Oddy's poems have been printed in the local papers, others have been issued in slip form for presentation purposes. Mr. Oddy is a prophet not without honour even in his own country. In

acknowledging a copy of some of his verses, the Venerable Archdeacon
Musgrave, of Halifax, wrote him as follows :—" Many thanks for your
poetry and the rich treasure it contains."

On one occasion, now nearly thirty years ago, Mr. Oddy visited
Chatsworth, and subsequently wrote a descriptive poem entitled
"Lines on a Visit to Chatsworth." He forwarded a copy to His
Grace the late Duke of Devonshire, and was fortunate enough to
receive the following autograph letter in reply :

DEVONSHIRE HOUSE, PICCADILLY, LONDON, W.
SIR,   MAY 21ST, 1868.
  I am much obliged to you for sending me your poetry on Chatsworth. I
duly received your letter while I was at Temple Newsome, and in compliance
with your wishes I gave one of the copies to Sir Wm. Knollys, Comptroller to
the Prince of Wales, and requested him to lay it before His Royal Highness.
                                I remain, yours obediently,
MR. JOHN ODDY.   DEVONSHIRE.

Lines on the Last Hawthorn in Whitcliffe Lane.

IN Whitcliffe lane for fifty years,
    I've stood cold winter's bitter blast ;
Seen many changes, many tears :
    My friends are gone, and I'm the last.

From Bandwalk gate to Maltkiln end,
    Protected by an old stone wall ;
Our line of hawthorns did extend,
    Full six feet broad, and very tall.

The sparrows in our midst have fought,
    And rais'd up many a chirping row ;
The robin here has shelter sought :
    The blackbird and the passing crow.

Each spring-time did our buds invite ;
    Cover'd our boughs with leaves of green :
Deck'd out our twigs with bloom snow-white ;
    A finer hedgerow scarce was seen.

The boys oft climbed us for a flower
    To grace their coat, or trim their cap :
The girls made wreaths to deck their bower ;
    Each broke off bloom, or marr'd our sap.

In summer-time we've often lent
    Our shade to weary passers-by,
And many a grateful heart has sent
    Thanks to our God, who rules on high.

Poor invalids, both young and old,
   Have sat beneath us many an hour,
And to the strong their stories told,
   Whilst shelt'ring from a passing shower,

At eventide all down the lane,
   Our bloom with fragrance fill'd the air;
When wash'd by cooling showers of rain :
   Or deck'd with pearly dewdrops fair.

In autumn, too, when nights were long,
   And gentle breezes fann'd the air,
The sparrow gave his notes of song ;
   The bat, the glow-worm, too, were there.

The clocks rang out the hours of time ;
   The moon gave out her pale dim light :
Fond lovers sat beneath our shrine,
   And each to each their vows did plight.

In autumn, too, our haws did form,
   As food for birds, in time of snow,
Ripe fruit for winter's bitter storm :
   Their wants did their Creator know.

But now the field has all been sold,
   And houses built upon the land ;
My mates are gone, and I am told
   That I have not so long to stand.

No whirr of wheels, no whistling boys,
   No workmen to draw out the line ;
No shouting "make a less yer noise :"
   Hold up!" "be steady!" how you twine.

Then farewell ! Wrathmell, Rhodes and you,
   The lads, the wheels, and Sambo too ;
Farewell ! to scenes of youth so true,
   To all, I now must bid adieu !

My Old Anvil Block.

AND now with a portion of this my old block,
In conclusion I write a few lines from my stock ;
With pleasure I've written the subject in hand,
About the old block, where my anvil did stand.

From facts I have told you the place where it stood,
'Twas opposite Fulneck down in the north wood;
But like finite man, its beauty was doom'd,
To the axe of the woodman who now lays entom'b.
Four horses to teagle, by six horses drawn,
This once lordling oak from the forest was torn;
For millwrights who of it an axletree made,
For a huge water-wheel, to drive on the cloth trade
In Cockersdale Valley.   On boulders it ran,
On boulders for brasses and that was the plan,
And for many long years by water 'twas turned,
Till the mill went to rack, and this wheel was then spurn'd.
Many rounds it had turn'd, without thoughts or fears,
Midst the trials and changes of many long years.
But man in his changes and chances of life,
Is many times turned by affection or strife.
Of the axle a part, in time, fell to me,
A block I made of it, till my course I could see.
Two years I work'd o'er it, and good lessons learn'd
Of practical life, whilst my horse shoes I turn'd;
As a relic I priz'd it, 'twas good British oak,
The heart that was left, was still firm as a rock;
But been mortis'd and weather'd, hammer'd and burn'd,
My shop too removed, and a new block I'd earn'd;
Its place was supplied by a new one in stock,
As its firmness was gone, for a good anvil block.
But as monuments rais'd o'er heroes of worth,
And men who have honour'd the land of their birth;
Even I have thought fit of this old block to make,
Some token of love and respect for its sake;
Some hafts and gag handles, I've made for my trade,
A bloodstick, etc., they'll save life if they're made.
For the first four officers, I've made from the block,
A penholder each, for a pen and its sock;
Those holders I've giv'n, one may yet hold a pen,
To display forth the worth of the Westgate Hill men,
In whose company I've mix'd for the last seven years,
And am come once again to bid them what cheers.
May they still persevere with the work they've in hand,
To train up the young in their own native land;
May they firmly as ever all pull at one string,
And their mental society a rich harvest bring.
May I, too, still work hard, be firm as a rock,
And for ever remember my old anvil block.

On Music.

In music, one joy of my life and my heart,
How oft I have long'd to take my own part
From my earliest youth and even till now,
Its charms I have lov'd and striven to know.
In minor and major, its wonderful themes,
Have taken my thoughts out to both extremes.
The former how touching, so mournful and sad,
Portrays our best thoughts, in rich music clad;
The latter more cheering, and lively, and gay,
For chorus or song on a bright May-day.
How often has poetry, strengthened by song,
Made words still more joyous, when sung by the strong.
How often my thoughts have been melted in tears
By songs I've heard sung in bygone years.
How oft have my hairs been set on an end,
When the full flowing chorus to heaven did ascend.
And now for a period of full fifty years,
Its charms I've enjoyed amid hopes and fears.
'Tis all we can take with us, out of the world
May we still cling to it, with our banners unfurl'd.

Lines on Love.

Oh! what is Love, that glows so in the heart?
That God-like tie, that will not let minds part—
That secret principle, so charming from within—
That mystery to man, in life so woven in?
The spell of life which buoys up all our hopes,
And bears us up in joy, or disappointment's strokes.
At birth, the infant doth this tie receive,
And love reciprocates ere it begins to live.
We well may ask, how does it spring, and whence—
That infant smile of heavenly innocence?
'Tis Love, that bursts so freely from the heart,
The seat and source of which we only know in part.
To parents, labouring on and scarcely knowing why,
Their youthful flock to rear, all seems infinity;
But yet a tie is there, which none can move—
A father's centre'd hopes, a mother's love.
Would God that all their future life could be,
One hallow'd course of joy, and true simplicity.

Our Town Hall Clock and Chimes.

A GOOD, sound bell in key of D—
　In bells a fre'er note than C—
Full thirty hundredweight 'twould be:
　Just like the Mirfield tenor.

For Cambridge chimes you would want four:
　A, B, C sharp, and Upper E.
They sound much nicer in a tower,
　But price would run accordingly.

A good, strong clock—why not say two?—
　To ring the chimes and turn the hands;
Give number one the hours when due,
　Or both in combination stand.

THE OLD BRITISH SCHOOL, CLECKHEATON, WHICH STOOD ON THE
SITE OF THE PRESENT TOWN HALL.

A downward blow I'd give each bell,
　As better than the under-jerk;
A spring would help the tone to swell—
　Require less power to do the work.

The dial shafts black ebony,
　Expansion and corrosion nil:
The lightning might not pass, you see,
　And us with disappointment fill.

A tocsin bell I'd place above,
  With a free swinging motion :
In times of danger it would prove
  A source of true devotion.

NEW TOWN HALL, CLECKHEATON.

It might call out our volunteers
  As body-guard of some tried friend,
Who, with golden key, would move the bars,
  And a *fue de joie* the air would rend.

Inside, we have a splendid hall,
  Bespeaking local enterprise ;
May no rude hand be rais'd at all
  To mar it or to minimise.

We cannot vie with Notre Dame
  In its high tow'rs and carrillon ;
But quite content with what we see—
  What some have wish'd to open free,
  In honour of the Jubilee,
    Our new and grand Town Hall.

The Royal Standard grace thy tower,
  No faction fights for ever seen ;
Peace and goodwill maintain the power,
  Of this our good and noble Queen.

FRANK PEEL.

By CHAS. F. FORSHAW, LL.D.

FRANK PEEL was born on the 29th May, 1831, at Great Horton, near Bradford, and was the son of Mr. Edward Peel, a Worsted Manufacturer at that place. He served his apprenticeship with Mr. Fred Hinings, Draper, Bradford, and married in 1856, Harriet Emma, the sister of the latter gentleman, and second daughter of Mr. William Hinings of Pudsey. On his marriage he entered into partnership with his brother-in-law, and they commenced business at Heckmondwike as Linen Drapers &c., the style of the firm being Hinings and Peel. This partnership lasted for some years, but eventually Mr. Hinings went out, and Mr. Peel continued to do a good business in the old shop, in the market place, for thirty years, besides which, he held the post of Editor of the *Heckmondwike Reporter* for fourteen or fifteen years of that period. In 1886 he relinquished the drapery business, and entered into partnership with Mr. Albert Senior, on the death of the latter's father, Mr. Thomas Wilby Senior, who had conducted the *Heckmondwike Herald* from the 19th October, 1877, assisted by Mr. Peel. Under Mr. Peel's editorship the paper has been very successful, and much enlarged. Five different editions are published every Thursday evening, viz.: the *Heckmondwike Herald*, the *Mirfield Herald*, the *Birstall Herald*, the *Thornhill Herald*, and the *Spen Valley Times*. There have appeared from time to time many most interesting articles on antiquarian subjects from Mr. Peel's able and prolific pen. Amongst these may be mentioned a long series of chapters on "Old Liversedge" (begun on the 14th May, 1886, and concluded 28th October, 1887). "The Rising of the Luddites," first appeared in the *Herald*, prior to its publication in book form in 1880, a much enlarged edition of which was issued in 1886. Mr. Peel's latest work is entitled "Nonconformity in the Spen Valley," 1891. He is at at present engaged in revising and extending, (in fact re-writing) the "Old Liversedge" articles which will be incorporated with other papers, and will shortly be issued under the title of

" Spen Valley: Ancient and Modern." It would be endless to give a complete list of Mr. Peel's prose works, but mention may be made of one or two serials which he has given to the public viz.: " Cavaliers and Roundheads, or the Neviles of Liversedge Hall," " Oakwell Hall, and the Fair Maid of Birstall," " The Battle of Towton Field," and many other historical papers have also appeared in the columns of the *Herald*.

Our readers will judge from the above brief sketch of Mr. Peel, that he has been an active worker in the prose walks of literature and from the specimens of his verse quoted they will see that he has also wandered within the boundaries of the rich meadow-lands of poetry, and culled sweet garlands of its choicest flowers. No one has done so much to perpetuate Spen Valley history as Mr. Peel—and no one better deserves a place among its bards than this genial and gifted gentleman. We have only just touched the fringe of his garment as it were in giving these records of his busy career—many more facts of absorbing interest might be given, but in a work of this nature, owing to want of space, we are reluctantly compelled to considerably curtail the memoir.

Benedicite.

MAY thy life be ever happy,
  May its course be one of joy,
Full of ever-varying pleasure,
  And of bliss without alloy.
May thy spirit ever hopeful
  Never yield to dark despair,
May thy beauty ne'er be blighted
  By the withering hand of care.

Wherever thou dost wander
  May contentment be thy lot,
And like the verdant ivy
  Cling firmly round thy cot.
May thy brow be never clouded,
  May thine eye be ever clear,
And may none but gladsome tidings
  Ever break upon thine ear.

May thy pilgrim way be lighted
   With the brightness from above,
May thou bask in mid-day splendour
   Of the radiant sun of love ;
May the drooping form of sorrow
   Ne'er assail thy gentle breast
But a cheerful, loving spirit
   Ever there securely rest.

May the bigot's cloud of darkness
   Ne'er obscure thy reason's light ;
May the scales of superstition
   Ne'er obstruct thy mental sight.
May thy heart be e'er the centre
   Where all gentle feelings meet,
And may dark and frenzied passion
   Ne'er usurp its judgment seat.

May angel hands attend thee
   Ever constant, ever near
Ever wave their bright wings o'er thee
   Nothing doubt thee, nothing fear ;
And when glimpses of a future
   Makes thee tire of earthly joys,
When thou'rt weary of its tinsel
   Its vanities and noise :

When thy happy spirit flutters
   In its prison house of clay,
Hears in fancy heavenly voices
   Softly calling thee away,
May the same bright forms watch o'er thee
   Making light the bed of death ;
And may all thou love'st be near thee
   As thou yield'st thy fleeting breath !

In Memoriam.

Moor'st thou thy little bark so soon ?
The waves of life have scarce begun
To ripple round the structure frail,
No adverse wind has bent its sail :

Yet silently with muffled oar,
Thou seek'st in haste yon radiant shore,
And pilots from the haven come—
Bright heavenly forms—to guide thee home.

Yet wherefore haste so soon away,
Sweet little voyager, oh say ?
Dread'st thy frail bark the tempest's shock—
The treacherous sand—the sunken rock ?
With prophet's vision pierced thine eye
The shades of dim futurity !
Heard'st thou the noise of far-off strife—
The wild instinctive fight for life,
Where the strong trample down the weak,
And truth in vain a rest doth seek—
Where man to Mammon bows the knee
In undisguised idolatry ?
Saw'st thou all this, then turned thine helm,
In dread some wave might thee o'erwhelm ?
Fearful of earth-taint leaped thy soul,
With joy to reach so soon its goal,
And join the bright and radiant throng,
Who sing the everlasting song.

God speed thine everlasting flight !
Gone—e'er the canker or the blight
Had robbed the flow'ret of its bloom,
And wasted all its rich perfume !
Gone—e'er thy form has reached its prime,
Or e'er the iron hand of time
Had slowly crushed and seared thy soul :
Or e'er the guilt-stained world had stole
The priceless gem of innocence—
Too oft, alas ! a frail defence
Against the many snares and wiles
That unsuspicious youth beguiles.

Death wins not oft so fair a prize
As now in his cold embrace lies :
Though at his touch the roses fled,
And slowly drooped the willing head—
Though he the beating heart hath stilled,
And its warm current fast congealed—
Though now the speaking eye is hid,
And firmly sealed the curtained lid—

That the pure soul no more may shine
And flash from those twin orbs of thine—
Though o'er the brightly polished brow
Unearthly pallor settles now—
Though on thy ruby lips is set
The spoiler's seal of silence,—yet
He hath not from thy pale face driven
That smile—the sign and seal of heaven !

Now calmly lies thy little head ;
Warm falls the sunlight on thy bed ;
'Bove the green-sward no stones arise,
To tell who underneath them lies ;
A simple sod—for thee more meet
Than all the pageants of the great.
No mournful requiem hast thou, save
The wind that moans around thy grave,
And the tall bending poplar tree,
Waving in solemn symphony.

No need hast thou of mournful lays,
Engraved on stone, to sound thy praise :
A better emblem could not grace
Thy verdant, lonely resting place,
Than the sweet daisy, peeping low,
That round thy little grave doth grow,
Which opes its petals to the sun,
And, when his radiant course is run,
Shuts them against the noxious shade,
And stoops for shelter 'neath the blade
Of grass, which forms its canopy,
And shelters it from injury,
From nipping frosts and steeping dew,
Till beaming day shall call anew
Its budding beauties forth once more,
And find them brighter than before.
'Tis nature's monument ! Naught here
Can raise the bitter jest or sneer
That often greets the empty state
And titles of the moulding great.

How, from such rich and storied urns,
The sickening soul most gladly turns
To gaze upon the verdant glade,
Where now thy little form is laid.

·Though not in consecrated ground,
Thy sleep for that is not less sound ;
Nor 'neath the shade of gothic pile—
Nor 'neath the dim Cathedral aisle ;
A loftier dome is reared o'er thee,
The broad heaven is thy canopy !

The Priest and the Robber.

A SPANISH robber chief, by name Don José,
    Finding that prey scarce on the hills had grown,
Rather than starve, crept from his cave so cosy,
    And cautiously drew near the neighbouring town,
Devoutly hoping that no curious eyes
Might chance to penetrate his thick disguise.

'Twas evening, and the vesper bells were sending
    Their solemn music through the balmy air,
And crowds of worshippers were slowly bending
    Their pious footsteps towards the house of prayer,
Each with a grave and very solemn look,
As if to worship really was no joke.

Don José mingled with the grave procession,
    And crossed devoutly at the temple door,
Then joined the wailing group who made confession,
    On bended knees, upon the hard stone floor,
Hoping to merit future worlds of bliss
By suffering self-inflicted woes in this.

Around the Virgin blazed some scores of tapers,
    Flooding with light the temple quaint and old,
And crowds of shaven priests were cutting capers
    Around a table piled with glittering gold,
For masses paid to raise from purgatory
Unready souls up to the realms of glory.

This heap of gold quite struck Don José's fancy ;
    With greedy eyes he viewed the prospect rare,
And wished that he, by some power of necromancy,
    Could safe transport it to his mountain lair,
Thinking, no doubt, that such a great temptation
Might make the holy priests forget their station.

But how to get it was a weighty query, -
  Which put Don José in a wondering dream,
And set him pondering, till with planning weary,
  He hit at last upon a likely scheme,
And straightway rose to put his sage conclusion,
Like a good general, into execution. .

Roused from his reverie, our friend Don José
  Looked round and found the people all were gone,
Except a jolly priest, all fat and rosy,
  Who sat in the communion all alone.
In well-feigned horror at some sad transgression,
José fell down and to him made confession :

"Oh, holy father, hear my sad narration,
  A hideous crime weighs down my guilty soul :
I'm lost! I'm lost! I fear beyond salvation,
  And doomed in torment evermore to howl !
The very earth my guilty foot seems spurning !
Cain's mark of blood is on my forehead burning."

" Be calm, my son," replied the holy father,
  " Spend not thy time in useless wail and plaint,
And sad and dreary lamentation—rather
  Humbly confess and faithfully repent :
Thy sin, though fearful, yet may be forgiven,
And thy dark soul absolved may enter heaven."

" Thanks," José cried, " thy words of consolation
  Fall on my spirit like some soothing balm,
And still my guilty bosom's perturbation,
  As sprinkled oils the surging billows calm.
Now listen, father, to my gloomy story,
My tale so dark, so hideous and so gory.

" The sun had sunk beyond yon frowning mountain,
  Like a huge ball of fire into the sea,
When near where springs the ever-bubbling fountain,
  I heard strange sounds of mirth and revelry,
Three priests it was, returning from Esterré,
Whose sparkling wine had made them rather merry.

" Impelled by hunger—fiercely did I stifle
  The fear that made my heart convulsive bound,
And at the first pointed my deadly rifle—
  The mountain caves sent back the hollow sound,

Another instant—and the wretch was lying,
Stretched near his mule, gasping for breath, and dying."

"Oh wretched man !" exclaimed the sage confessor,
"That tale of horror chills my very soul ;
Yet courage—though thou'rt such a great transgressor,
The holy church has power to make thee whole.
Here with this scourge each day in humble posture
Chastise thyself and say a paternoster.

"Then, every morning at this shrine so holy,
Present an offering of a bright pistole,
That with a dirge of deepest melancholy
I here may pray that priest's unready soul,
Its failings and short-comings all forgiven,
May duly mingle with the saints in heaven."

"Hold! holy father," cried Don José, gazing
With gloating eyes once more upon the gold,
"This portion of my tale you deem amazing,
I've got a darker sequel to unfold."
"*Worse than to kill a priest !* What can it be ?"
"Father," said Don José, "I did slay all three !"

"Horror!" exclaimed the startled friar, rising.
"Father," cried José, "hear me out I pray.
What I've already said may seem surprising,
But yet I've something more I fain would say.
Since I that blood upon the mount did spill
I'm tempted every priest I see to kill !

"Even as I speak I feel the strange temptation
Holding within my breast no doubtful strife ;
Fly ! I implore you, without hesitation,
This instant, if you'd save your precious life."
Then springing up, José stood sternly facing
The monk, with grins and gestures most menacing.

The frightened monk made several unavailing
Attempts to open the communion door,
But could not—so he boldly leaped the railing
And ran as he had never run before,
While José, with a merry peal of laughter,
Picked up the gold—and quietly followed after.

MISS ALICE G. RHODES,

By ALBERT E. ELLISON, M.D.S.

THIS young lady, who resides at Mount Villa, Heckmondwike, is the daughter of Josiah Rhodes, Esq., of that town. She has made many charming contributions in poetry to the local press, either under her own name or a *nom de plume*. The poem on " Spring " first appeared in the *Cleckheaton Guardian*, and was awarded a prize by the editor of that paper. The editor characterizes it of " especial merit, abounding with charming sentiments and portrayed in language which does the author great credit."

Spring.

Oh! Spring! Oh! lovely Spring!
In all thy beauteous charms do we rejoice,
And e'er delight to welcome thy dear voice
  With longing hearts and ever-watchful list'ning.
When earth throws off her wintry garb of white,
Then everything bursts forth with new delight
  To lovely growth : in brightest radiance glist'ning.
Oh! Spring! Oh! charming Spring!

Oh! Spring! Oh! hopeful Spring!
The happy watchword for a plenteous year,
Which bids us hope, not deigning aught to fear,
  Throughout the days and months that are forthcoming.
Awaken'd life in all the joy of youth
Must join in shewing forth that Nature's truth
  Doth now assert itself in garb becoming
To Spring! Oh! cheerful Spring!

Oh! Spring! Oh! happy Spring!
The birds in sweetest notes now sing to thee
Their rippling melodies from budding tree,
  Or like the lark to heav'nward turn their singing.
While here below earth shines with flowers so bright
As stars from heaven had come in the day-light,
  Some message of true life to mortals bringing
In Spring! Oh! wond'rous Spring!

Oh! Spring! Oh! joyous Spring!
An emblem of our lives in thee we find,
How darkest seasons may be left behind,
  And life be ever towards the harvest flowing.
While every year new beauties do unfold
Their loveliness. Yet still remains untold
  The wond'rous depth of Nature's rich bestowing
Of Spring! Oh! glorious Spring!

Life's Progress.

Each year, and day, and moment, as it goes,
Doth add its record to the list of those
　Which went before, to tell of progress new,
Some battle won, in science or in art,
Some new invention may have been a part
　Of clearer vision in a wiser few.

The work of every man is to provide
A wave of pleasure in the rushing tide
　Of life.　In hardest toil may come this thought,
That some will realise a great delight
By following their own duty's call aright
　To gain possession of the work he wrought.

Man works with man, how sweet the concord proves,
If one with heart and soul the other loves.
　Each one, with purpose fixed and standard high,
Will surely lengthen progress' pathway, tho'
The stores of fruitful wealth he may not know
　In the small star he chanced to descry.

May not a few men's lives thereby be blest ?
Where influence of good works takes its rest
　We know not, or if ever such a thing
Could come to pass, for naught is lost to sight.
If ne'er so small the deed, the motive's right
　'Twill counted be in our world's reckoning.

As light from heavenly bodies on their way
Take time, and reach us at some distant day,
　So wisdom from its high remotest source
Cast faintest glimmers through long ages past,
Then each ray gathers more, till at the last
　A cloud of light descends the downward course.

Yet it is upward that the progress moves
As each discovered wonder clearly proves
　That to a height beyond all ken of man
Progression aims, not with a sudden blow,
But wheel in wheel, revolving in a slow
　Rotation.　This the universal plan.

As now we see how far advanced we are
From what we were, so may be change as far
　Between the present and a future time.
The high estate to which the progress leads
We call perfection.　But that blest state needs
　A Power beyond, which is o'er all sublime.

SAMUEL DRAKE ROBERTS.

By CHAS. F. FORSHAW, LL.D.

MR. ROBERTS, who for many years past has resided at 'Tenlands,' Gomersal, was born at Bradford on the 26th of January, 1832. He is the author of "Stansfield: A Tragedy," pp. 80, published at Heckmondwike in 1864. In addition to having been the creator of this volume, which we have recently had the pleasure of perusing, and which is prolific with powerful passages, Mr. Roberts has made many pleasing contributions to local periodicals. We quote one on the death of the Rev. R. F. Taylor, M.A., who for fifty years was vicar of the Old White Chapel, Cleckheaton. We also cull an extract from "Stansfield."

"Stansfield."

A TRAGEDY.   ACT IV. SCENE II. P. 67.

ARTHUR (*after sighing deeply*)—All, all is hollow: everything
    a farce
From first to last.   Fame, riches, rank and honour—
Ay, all distinctions that the world can offer—
Light as the frothy crests of ocean-waves!
Poor, paltry bubbles on a phantom sea,
Though springs which partly urged me on to deeds
For which the final sentence is to be
Damnation—utter and unmitigated:
That's it—the finishing-up-stroke, crowning all
And then—no pause, no rest, no hope, no end;
But dull old Time will idly wander on—
On through the measureless ages, till engulfed
In the wide jaws o' the desert of eternity!
But can a passing moment's brief duration
Fix deeds which merit such a deathless death?
Away—away the thought! I'll not believe it!
It is a lie—a gross and palpable lie,
Forged by a cunning priesthood to enslave
The asses of mankind.   Let me look round
And mark the aspect of this mundane sphere,
With twice ten thousand thousand forms of life,
All bound together by unerring laws

Which never miss their object.   Can it be
That He—the Founder of this planet's structure,
The great originating one (whose power
Sent forth the high irrevocable mandate
That perfect order and celestial beauty
Should spring from lifeless elements, and it was so,;
He but an uncontrollable Despot whose dire cruelty
No tongue could shadow forth ?   Away such nonsense !
It is an insult to the living God
Who in His wisdom made us what we are !
No, no ! let reason be my guiding star,
And whisper that, however black the deed,
What's done in Time, in Time receives its meed.
                        Scene closes.

In Memoriam.

THE REV. R. F. TAYLOR, WHITE CHAPEL, CLECKHEATON.

A GOOD man hath departed
    From earth and earthly things :
And heavenward hath started
    To meet the King of Kings.
A blameless life is ended,
    A life of hope and trust,
Of love and duty blended—
    Alas ! to end in dust !

The chapel bell is tolling :
    A sorrowing throng is seen :
The mourning cars are rolling
    Towards the solemn scene.
And many an eye is bleared and dim,
    And many a cheek is wet,
And many a prayer ascends for him
    Whose earthly sun hath set.

For recollection moulds him—
    Yea. moulds him as before ;
And memory yet beholds him,
    Beholds him as of yore.
Beholds the pale, angelic face—
    Beholds the upward look—
Beholds him as he spake of grace,
    The Message and the Book.

There was a daily beauty
That sanctified his life ;
And fifty years of duty
To mend a world of strife ;
To preach forgiveness to the weak ;
To beckon goodness on ;
To humble pride : the Tempter seek
And bid him to be gone !

All hushèd are the voices
Within that ancient fane ;
Save one that should rejoice us,
For we die to rise again :
The emblems of mortality
Are in this house of prayer—
The coffin crowned with wreaths we see ;
The honoured dust is there.

Near that eastern window standing
Is our Saviour, Light and Word :
And near, with mien commanding,
Stands the Prophet of the Lord.
One softly speaks of heavenly love :
One thunders out the law ;
One gently leads his flock above ;
The other strikes with awe.

And prayer and benediction
In that reverend pile are heard,
Speaking comfort to affliction,
Which may pine with hope deferred.
Listen to the organ pealing !
Listen as the voices rise !
Till the harmony is stealing
Through the building to the skies.

Then the good man's dust is taken
To the consecrated earth ;
And many hearts are shaken
That such piety and worth
Will not again be seen of men ;
For he, whom we deplore,
Has vanished from our mortal ken,
And vanished evermore.

M. A. STEAD.

By CHAS. F. FORSHAW, LL.D.

THE following verses originally appeared in the *Cleckheaton Guardian*, in June, 1880, above the initials "M.A.S." I am unable to give any particulars of the authoress, beyond that for some time she was engaged as a teacher at some school in Wyke.

Attachment to the English Church.

My Mother Church! It may not be,
But I must ever cling to thee
With feelings of a trusting child
To parent ever fond and mild.
While men, misguided, start away,
And proudly spurn thy gentle sway,
More simply to thy fold I'd turn,
More humbly from thy lips I'd learn.

They say that on thy brow appears
The wrinkle of declining years ;
That weary is thy honour'd head,
And all thy pristine vigour fled.
But no! The youthful eagle's flight
Is glorious in the noontide light ;
Yet rolling years behind her soar,
With eye undazzled as before.

The mocking laugh some love to raise,
To point the finger of dispraise,
From blemishes to tear the veil,
And joyful tell the well-conn'd tale ;
But will they dare to lift a hand
Against the glory of our land—
Our Church, whose noble army stood
And sealed them witness with their blood?

No! Though the cry is echoing round—
" Down with her even to the ground !"
Though thunders from apostate Rome,
In muffled guise, against her come,
Our hearts, O aged parent, move
With the quick bound of grateful love ;
We circle round thee to defend
Our father's pride, our country's friend.

We tremble not, our cause is high,
To God we lift the prayerful eye ;
Calmly we mark the rushing foe,
The standard of our Lord we know ;
We see His banner o'er us wave,
We feel that He is strong to save ;
And while we know a Saviour near,
The might of man we cannot fear.

THE OLD CROSS AT OAKENSHAW, NEAR CLECKHEATON.

MISS JANE TAYLOR.

By JOSEPH N. CUTTS, Ph.D. B.Sc.

ASSOCIATE OF THE PHARMACEUTICAL SOCIETY AND DOCTOR
OF DENTAL SURGERY.

THIS young lady is the sister of the late Mr. T. Birkby Taylor, whose biography, etc., commences on page 180. She is the second daughter of Mr. Joseph Taylor, and resides at Westfield Cottage, Wyke. She was born at Cleckheaton on August 11th, 1866, and educated at the Moravian Schools, Wyke, and Fairfield, Manchester. Miss Taylor has been a prolific writer of verse, but with a wisdom, rarely met with in youth, she has always been chary of publishing. Among the papers she has contributed to are the *Yorkshire Weekly Post*, the *Halifax Mercury*, the *Dewsbury Chronicle*, the *Cleckheaton Guardian*, the *Bradford Mercury*, and the *Leeds Times*.

Something More.

THINKING on a midnight dreary, when the world should
   aye be cheery—
Why the world is never cheery to a person rich or poor.
Why the world is never cheery, but is always sad and weary,
Ever dreary to the soul who on his woes doth sadly pore.
Thus I murmured—"This the mystery, that he longs for
   something more—
     Ever yearns for 'Something more!'"
There's the infant weak and helpless—much more like a
   bundle shapeless—
Often whining till you wish it anywhere outside the door.
If by any chance it's pleasant, sure it worries each one
   present,
Causing them to pay attentions to a thing they think a bore,
Wondering how it is that man is ever such an awful bore,
     Till the infant cries for more.

And if baby's thoughts can wander, and the tiny mind can
    ponder,
Surely this would be its pondering as it sits upon the floor:
Or in handsome cradle lying, perhaps the future man is
    sighing :—
"Though I have so much that's lovely, yet an absence I
    deplore ;
Though my father's all I wish for, though my mother I
    adore,
        Still I long for 'Something more !' "

Then a few years pass so lightly o'er the head of one who
    brightly
Takes the gifts the gods provide, which means for him a
    goodly store ;
There is nothing he can sigh for ; he has nothing left to
    cry for ;
Every want is well supplied or ever he his wish outpour—
Toys and books, and playmates handy, gems of earth, and
    sea, and shore—
        He can wish for nothing more.

See, she sits in state receiving all the gifts her friends are
    leaving ;
She is Queen on this her birthday, and she tells them all
    she's four—
Toys innumerable bringing, little guests around her singing
Laughing gaily, all her presents strewed about upon the
    floor—
Suddenly remembers something that she cried for days
    before,
        And *must have* that "Something more."

Well equipped for school, he started, handsome, manly,
    proud, light-hearted,
Trunks well packed with best of garments, and of sweets
    and cakes a store ;
Books, and playthings scientific, chemicals the most terrific,
Which his poor fond mother frightened. Oh, the agony
    she bore
When he nearly blew the house down ! And she heard
    him thro' the door
        Gently murmur "Just once more !"

See him and his friends together in the dull and wintry
    weather ;
He is chosen as the *Speaker*—he the mighty man of lore—
Hear him speak of " Upper Classes," " How to Elevate
    the Masses,"
" Individualism," " Republics,"—all his father said before
Jumbled up and given at random, till they pitch him on
    the floor,
        Crying, " Give us something more ! "

Equally the girl is starting well in school life—even parting
From the dolls and toys and playmates she had loved so
    dear before ;
Trunks well lined with all to please her ; no one even
    tries to tease her ;
Surely never was a girl who had such pleasures e'er before,
Never was a girl so happy in all ages gone before :
        She can want but little more.

Yes, the school is very jolly, and her dearest friend is
    " Dolly " ;—
Dolly's father is an Earl's son—in distinctions to the fore
Girls flock round the one so pretty, though they never
    thought her witty,
And the girl who gets the prizes is the one *they* think a bore.
Still, the prizes would be glory—this she had not thought
    before—
        There, you see, that " Something more ! "

Schooldays now are over fairly, and we see the youth so
    rarely
Gifted with all worldly goods and mental gifts—if nothing
    more—
Influence not long is wanted ; each unspoken wish is
    granted ;
Rich friends flock around him gaily, spendthrift friends
    his aid implore ;
He has powers, and he can use them :—what could any
    wish for more ?
        He wants nothing—nothing more.

M

Does he say so as he dances, as his spirited charger prances,
As he sings and jokes so gaily with his friends and many
    more ?
As he labours at his writing, he would rather be inditing
Sonnets to a high-born maiden, whom to see was to adore,
But the lady tells him truly she's his friend and nothing
    more ?
    And he moans, "Oh, *nothing* more ?"

Schooldays for the girl are over, and she revels now in
    clover,
Dancing is most charming when you've partners and a good
    spring floor.
She had that.   And many others would have left the
    fondest mothers
Had the fates spread such inducements in their way—oh,
    what a store !—
All she asked for, all she thought of, at her feet delight to
    pour
    Those who love her more and more.

Young and handsome, tall and slender, dressed in faultless
    taste and splendour,
Art allied with Nature's charms succeed in making a *furore*.
For her hand such wealth is proffered ; talent, worth, and
    rank are offered
To the girl who sees beneath as one sees through an open
    door—
To a girl who learns to love, and wants that Love and
    nothing more—
    Only Love ? And *nothing* more ?

Middle-aged, and rich and stately, who was never seen till
    lately
With a frown upon his brow, but bright and free as e'er of
    yore.
How can he have ought to grieve him—he whose friends
    will never leave him
While his money lasts, and Fortune smiles at them from
    out his door ?
High position, wealth and power, wife and children to
    adore,
    Surely he can't ask for more !

In his library he ponders, and his eye full often wanders
Round the walls where range his treasures, and he cons
    them o'er and o'er ;
Wonders why that speculation caused him at the time
    elation
When he only staked three thousand (£3,000) and he might
    have made it *four.*
Works himself into a temper as he stamps along the floor.
Ah, alas! that "Something more!"

Comely still, and fair and haughty, well might she have
    passed for forty,
Though she must at least be *fifty*—friends their testimony
    bore.
Wealth and happiness can mellow what would be the "sere
    and yellow"
In a person favoured less by Fortune's overflowing store—
Ever flowing to the wight who has so much he can't want
    more !
        She has much—and *can't* want more !

But she *does*, and this her sorrow—which she thinks she
    has to borrow—
Still *she* thinks it *is* a sorrow for *her* daughter to be *poor.*
For the darling girl *will* marry, and has heart enough to
    carry,
All her points through opposition, such as she ne'er faced
    before.
"Twenty thousand" is her fortune, and her lover they call
    "*poor.*"
        He has BRAINS—and *little more !*

So I mused, and sadly poring on these problems—vainly
    soaring,
Then deep sifting all the mysteries that but grow to more
    and more,
" *All is vanity,*" I muttered, "never truer word was uttered,
" Solomon in all his glory ever longed for something more ;
" And the cry through endless ages will be heard for
    evermore.
        " ' Life ! oh *Life* for *Something More !* '"

THOMAS BIRKBY TAYLOR.

By CHAS. F. FORSHAW, LL.D.

Mr. T. B. Taylor was born at Wyke, June 22nd, 1855. He was the eldest son of Mr. Joseph Taylor of that place, who now carries on business as a miller at Oakenshaw. Mr. Taylor was educated at the Moravian Schools, Fulneck, and brought up as a woollen merchant with Messrs. Bottomleys, of Bradford. Very early in life—in fact long before his school-days were over—young Taylor showed an aptitude for versifying, and when manhood had scarcely dawned he had for a considerable period been a contributor to some of the foremost journals of the day. Unfortunately, that grim monster death, early claimed him for his own, and after an illness extending over a period of two or three years, he died on the 12th of August, 1891. Whilst holding the responsible office as buyer of flannels and blankets to Messrs. Bottomleys he was taken seriously ill, and shortly afterwards he entirely lost his sight. On eminent oculists being consulted, they attributed his illness and loss of sight to the pernicious effluvia arising from the stoved goods he was constantly amongst. In spite of the best medical advice, and every care, the poor fellow never rallied, and thus a life which some years ago gave great promise has been prematurely terminated. In the walks of literature he was a devoted disciple, as many of our readers will no doubt remember from contributions they may have seen. His literary efforts assisted in brightening the pages of many papers. As a conversationalist deceased possessed rare qualities ; he was gifted with a good memory, and was well read, and he shed a brightness on any society he entered. Mr. Taylor had for many years been a contributor to the *Yorkshireman*, generally writing under the *nom de plume* of "Tom Seymour," and when his lamented death took place, the following paragraph appeared in that periodical :—"The death of Mr. T. Birkby Taylor come like a personal affliction to us of the *Yorkshireman*, for in years gone by, when in the pride and vigour of his days, he formed an acceptable and loyal member of our staff, and wielded a nimble, lively, and always picturesque pen." His best work was his satirical verses, some of which were very happy in conception, and telling in execution. He also wrote a series of articles for the *Observer Budget*, entitled " In Deep Waters," descrip-

tive of a voyage to South Africa ; and he also contributed largely to
the *Cleckheaton Guardian.* Tom Taylor possessed a happy social gift
and sympathetic qualities which endeared him to a large circle of
friends. As a clever reciter his services were always ready at the call
of charity. He was a member of the Harmony Lodge of Freemasons.
Mr. Taylor was married in March 1886, and left a widow but no family.
The interment took place on the 26th of June, at Lower Wyke, in the
quaintly old-fashioned cemetery belonging to the Moravians, of which
denomination the deceased gentleman was a member. The simple, but
none the less solemn, funeral of the Moravians was conducted in the
chapel and at the graveside by the Rev. F. Clemens. The funeral
cortège was attended by the following officers and members of the
Harmony Lodge of Freemasons, viz. :—Messrs. J. Wright, P.M., W.
R. Hinings, P.M., T. Norfolk, P.M., W. Kingdon, W.M., E·
Mackay, S.W., W. G. Stansfield, J.W., W. Moxon, Secretary, J.
Davis, G. Gamble, I. Pratt, Clifford, Gaunt. T. Tilley, Smithies,
Galpine, and Lawson. These gentlemen walked in processional order
from Westfield Cottage (the residence of the late gentleman's parents,
to the chapel, and added greatly to the impressiveness of the ceremony)
one particular touching tribute of respect being the customary casting
of sprigs of acacia upon the coffin in its last resting-place by each
member of the Order present according to seniority. A number of
beautiful wreaths were sent by the friends and relatives of the
deceased.

All the Joys of the Season.

To you, little bright eyes, you dear little pet,
     I wish all the joys of the season ;
Whether embryo dandy or baby coquette,
     I wish you the joys of the season .
Don't eat too much pudding, nor too much spice cake,
But laugh if you can till your little sides ache ;
Be happy, and from me this kindly wish take
     That you'll find some toys Christmas trees on.

To you, happy maiden, so lively and gay,
     I wish all the joys of the season ;
I hope you'll have everything just-your own way,
     And a fill of the joys of the season.
May dances be many, and partners be nice,
May this Christmas-tide be all sugar and spice ;

And may some young spark ask you with him to "splice,"
    And sweeten the joys of the season.

To you, my dear fellow, old friend of my youth,
    I wish all the joys of the season ;
I hope that the close of the year brings no rush,
    But fills you with joys of the season.
May the "missis" be blooming and children be well,
Of troubles and trials may this be the knell ;
May pleasure and fun rush upon you pell-mell,
    And bring all the joys of the season.

To you, dear old friend, in the "yellow and sere,"
    I wish all the joys of the season.
May Jack Frost be kindly, and not too severe,
    But let you enjoy this glad season.
And to each of my readers, be you woman or man,
Be you fair, be you foul, be you black, be you tan,
Be you radiant as Venus, repulsive as Pan,
Be you young, be you old, in the rear of the van,
Be you rich, be you poor, be you healthy or wan,
    I wish you the joys of the season.

My Queen.

No jewelled diadem is her's,
    No gemmed tiara decks her brow,
Her coronal of dark brown hair
    Is lovelier far than these I vow ;
No sceptre bears she in her hand,
    No symbol of her power is seen,
But still her sov'reignty I own,
    And humbly bow before my queen.

Her only kingdom is my life,
    My faithful heart her only throne,
Her lightest wish is sternest law,
    Her smile the signal that I own ;
Her sole regalia's beauty's charm,
    And not Golconda's gems, I ween,
Can add one touch of loveliness
    To her I'm proud to call my queen.

Her words fall on my listening ear
    Like strains of some sweet angel-psalm,

The troubled waters of my soul
  Her voice has power to soothe and calm ;
Her influence permeates my life,
  And fills me with a joy serene ;
To me the earth is heaven's reflex,
  And owes its glamour to my queen.

Ah ! queenie mine ; no selfish thought
  Attaints the loyalty I give ;
And all the guerdon that I crave
  Is but beneath your rule to live ;
I only ask to see your smile,
  To watch your bright eyes, changeful scene,
To listen to your gladsome voice,
  And love you, only you, my queen.

In Memoriam.*

'Tis thirty years since my old friend and I
  First clasped our little hands in friendly token ;
And thro' the years that since have flitted by,
  That youthful pledge has still remained unbroken.
Through boyhood's, youth's, and manhood's changing days,
  Our friendship never from its course departed ;
His rectitude, his genial, kindly ways
  Made him esteemed as one who was true-hearted ;
His troubles he with fortitude did bear,
  With charity his heart was overflowing ;
When good work was in hand he did his share,
  Lukewarmness or indifference never shewing.
My friend was one whom many people loved,
  For truth and virtue ruled his every action.
By tales of woe his heart was ever moved ;
  Coldness or deceit, for him, had no attraction ;
The dearest place on earth to him was home,
  For there the mainsprings of his life were centred ;
From there he never willingly would roam,
  And there no trouble he could stem ere entered.
But God has taken him, " His will be done,"
  And He to sorrowing friends this boon has given,
That when our journey through this world is run,
  We shall meet our friend, to part no more, in heaven.

*[This piece possesses a somewhat melancholy interest. It is the last com-
position of its talented author.—EDITOR.]

WILLIAM TODD.

By WILLIAM HEDGES HATTON, F.R.H.S.

AUTHOR OF "THE CHURCHES OF YORKSHIRE," EDITOR OF "THE
BRADFORD MERCURY," LATE EDITOR "BRADFORD
CHRONICLE AND MAIL," AND
"BRADFORD TIMES."

———

WILLIAM TODD is one of our Yorkshire poets of humble origin.
Horace never attempted to screen the fact that he was the son of an
emancipated slave, and Beranger often planted in the face of society
his lowly origin. Wm. Todd, even in these days when ancestry counts
for a good deal, is none "too proud to care from whence he came." He
was born at East Harsley, a hamlet near Northallerton, some sixty-five
years ago. He had not the advantage of much schooling, indeed, outside his own efforts, his education was seriously neglected. At eight
years of age he was sent into the fields to work, at eleven years of age
he was hired to a man who proved himself to be of a most tyrannical
nature. Under his control Wm. Todd passed a most unhappy twelve
months. As a boy, however, he manifested a great thirst for knowledge. He saved as much as he possibly could from his small earnings,
and with his limited capital he purchased useful books. By his own
close study he was soon able to spell out the English language. He
then made his first purchase which was Wesley's Notes on the New
Testament. He looked upon this book as a rich store of instruction.
No miser loved his gold more than William Todd loved Wesley's
Notes. He studied them under difficulties, for he had to secretly
convey the candle into his bedroom, and blind the window in the most
careful manner that his master might not detect the light. He often
continued his reading until the early hours of the morning. Then he
saved sufficient money to enable him to purchase Bishop Horne's work
on the Psalms. With this he felt that his store of knowledge was
richer still. Persevering with the same policy, he soon became the
possessor of " Sutcliffe's Commentary on the whole of the Bible." As
he once remarked, "What a mountain of a library I had now." About
this time he obtained a situation in a warehouse. His employer ordered
him to work on the Sabbath Day. He refused, with the usual conse-
quences. Then William Todd sat down for his "maiden effort"—

"Heaven's Boon and Earth's Bliss." His work was favourably reviewed by Dr. Cook in the *Wesleyan New Connexion Magazine*. Thus encouraged, he wrote "The Footsteps of the Deity," which received a flattering notice from the pen of William Petty in the *Primitive Methodist Magazine*. Then followed in quick succession the following poems : "The Yorkshire Ploughman," "The Church," "The Fall of Sebastopol," "The Lily of the Valley," "The Rose of Sharon," "The Flower of Spen Valley," "Moses and his Critics," "A Satire : Jackey Dale." Subsequently William Todd produced a large collection of minor poems, which are too numerous for the mention of each title. Included in his collection are squibs on town matters, and these were often written amidst hard toil to obtain the means of subsistence, and frequently when his mind was troubled with affliction and loss. He has occasionally found pleasure in the study of the Greek poems, but in this relation not very much has come from his pen. When he was twenty years of age William Todd found himself located in Heckmondwike, where he still resides, and in which town all his publications have appeared.

An Echo from the Dales of the Plough.

SERENA, come and trace the steps of Him
Who spoke, and made immensity to teem
With worlds—unnumber'd worlds ; ah, see them rise,
And hang in ether blue,—in yonder skies.
But what a task ! 'twould take the life of man,
One moment of his history to scan ;
Nay, could he fly as swift as thought e'er flew,
From world to world, in yonder ether blue,
And wing his way in the vast field of space,
For twice ten thousand years, His steps to trace,
This tour so vast would not reveal an hour
Of the sublime production of His power.
As one system he view'd, another bright
Would be unveil'd to his astonish'd sight ;
When this he view'd, another then would rise,
Far, far away, to his admiring eyes ;
And thus 'twould be, could he pursue his way
Throughout a vast—a one eternal day :

Nay, should the glorious concourse of the sky,
Swifter than thought in all directions fly,
And ne'er return till every step they view,
The hills of bliss might bid them all adieu :
His steps so vast, vast as immensity,
One half to view would take eternity.
Then how shall I whose being's but finite,
E'er trace every step of the infinite,
Whose ways are deep, deep hid in mystery,
Whose vast existence spans eternity.

Here muse takes wing, where all the heavenly throng
And all the morning stars together sung ;
Where all was good, without a taint of crime,
Where vast eternity gave birth to time.

This, this the bound'ry where my muse can rove,
From error free, beyond a God of love ;
Ne'er nought reveal'd—here all is cloud and mist—
All that I know is this—He did exist,
Supremely good, supremely happy too—
This what's reveal'd to mortals here below.
How exercised His power, I cannot say ;
On fancy's pinions I might soar away,
And view in my excursion of surmise,
Worlds in succession rise and fall and rise,
Through ages vast, yea, through eternity :
But here I'm lost on an unbounded sea,
Then see, Serena, I His steps will trace,
As are marked out by nature's every grace :
Here goodness shines in earth, in air, in sky,
No place but where it meets the mortal eye,
And yet no place but where His wisdom shines,
Throughout His vast and glorious designs :
Sol pours his light, his light and heat benign ;
How vast the wisdom of this bright design !
Worlds vast whirl round this noble orb sublime,
Whirl, and have whirl'd thro' all the past of time :
All know their station, and all keep their sphere ;
None whirl too far, or ever pass too near ;
A deviation here with earth would be
Death to existence, both by land and sea ;
Earth would be frozen, or wear a parchèd dress,
And not as now be graced with every grace.

THOMAS WRIGHT.

By FRANK PEEL.

EDITOR OF THE "HECKMONDWIKE HERALD,"
AUTHOR OF "NONCONFORMITY IN THE SPEN VALLEY," "RISING
OF THE LUDDITES," "OLD LIVERSEDGE," "OLD
CLECKHEATON," ETC., ETC.

ON the north side of the hill facing the turnpike road leading from Cleckheaton to Hartshead Moor, stands an old farm-stead known as Lower Blacup. I believe there is no date on the building, but it is probably one of some antiquity, doubtless nearly 300 years old. It is still a good looking substantial house, and though some stones in the front show signs of decay, it will no doubt weather successfully the storms of another century. The house is prettily situated on the side of a hill, and although the neighbouring town is now creeping swiftly up to it, it is still a pleasant retired nook.

LOWER BLACUP, LIVERSEDGE, WHERE THOMAS WRIGHT RESIDED.

On May-day or there-abouts, in the year of our Lord 1767, this farm was taken by Mr. Thomas Wright, who at that time was just settling down in life. He was gifted with a powerful intellect, and

might have attained considerable literary eminence if he had received
a proper training. Unfortunately, he lost all his near relatives when he
was very young, and being left to the care of guardians who were un-
educated themselves and who placed no value upon learning, he was
suffered to grow up in comparative ignorance. In after life Thomas
Wright regretted that he was not under the care of some one in his
youth who could have appreciated the bent of his mind, but although
he had as good an excuse as any of his neighbours for living in ignorance he did not choose to do so. The craving for knowledge grew
with what it fed upon. He purchased books on all kinds of subjects,
read them with avidity, and being blessed with a prodigious memory
he soon found himself able to join in conversation with the most intel-
ligent people in the neighbourhood. As instance of the extraordinary
power he possessed of retaining what he read, I may state that it is
related by one who knew him well, that he could repeat the whole of
Milton's " Paradise Lost " whenever called upon, besides long selec-
tions from the works of other poets. A neighbour has also left it on
record that on the day when the *Leeds Mercury* (being a comparatively
small paper) arrived, Thomas Wright usually brought it with him to
his house, took a seat by the fire, and proceeded to read it through.
When he had once so read it, he could, if called upon immediately
afterwards, repeat the whole or any part of it even to an advertisement,
and so correctly that it was not necessary to refer to the paper itself.

With Thomas Wright's struggles as a tradesman I need not enter
as I am simply speaking of him as a literary man, nor need I dwell
upon his romantic courtship and subsequent elopement to Gretna
Green. His marriage was not a happy one, being embittered by un-
seemly bickerings with his wife's father and mother; ignorant
prejudiced people who never forgave him for marrying their daughter
clandestinely. I only name this latter episode in his life because it led
him into religious controversies with some of the leading writers of the
sect to which his father-in-law belonged, and into which controversy
he imparted much of the bitter feeling with which he came to regard
his wife's parents. For many years Thomas Wright was indeed the
champion of the Methodists in the locality, and right valiantly and
with hearty good will did he wield his keen weapons of wit and satire,
infuriating still more his wife's relatives who belonged to the most violent
Calvinistic sect. It does not appear that Wright was ever a member
of the Methodist Society himself, unless it was just at the close of his
life. Most of his answers to the Calvinistic pamphleteers were written
in rhyme and were immensely popular, some favourite portions being
stored in the memories of his admirers for a generation.

Many stories are still current in the locality where Wright lived
of his ready wit and courage, and many fragments of pieces of a

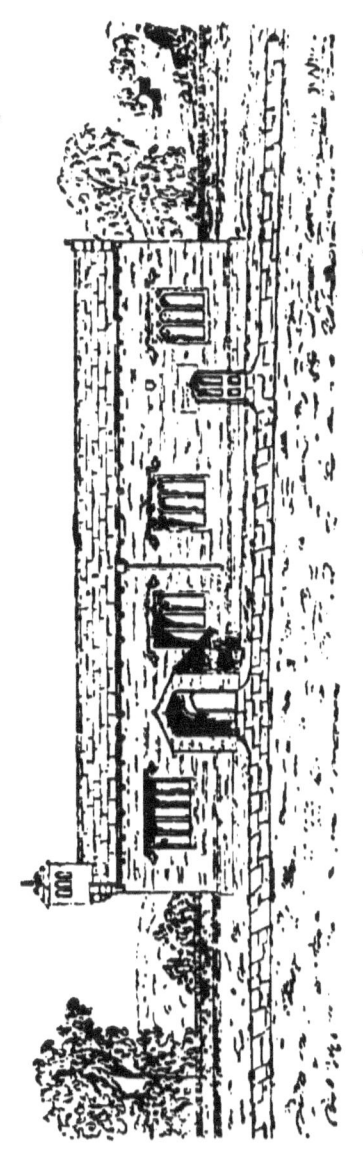

THE OLD WHITE CHAPEL, CLECKHEATON, AS IT WAS IN WRIGHT'S TIME.

humorous kind were repeated by old people many years after his death.
Wright was indeed a genial man.   His social qualities endeared him to
his neighbours, who esteemed his company, very highly, and were de-
lighted to listen to his lively and humorous fire-side talk.   He was a
great reader, and loved his quiet paper and his book, but he loved also
the company of his friends.   His life was chequered with many serious
troubles, and his sensitive mind was continually fretted and worried by
the petty malice of his first wife's relatives, but he was notwithstanding
all, no sour-faced ascetic, but possessed of a warm heart and was well
known as a friend and wellwisher to a wide and ever increasing circle,
who loved the man and admired his talents.   He has been accused of
being sarcastic, and it must be confessed there is some truth in the
charge ; his forte however was piquant wit and lively banter; he had
faults doubtless, as all mortals have, but he was withal a notable man
in his day and generation, a man of strong intellect and great force of
character.   The motives which led him into the arena of theological
controversy were perhaps not always pure, but he did yeoman service
on behalf of a feeble flock, and is well worthy of honour.   He died
January 30th, 1801, of an attack of typhus fever, aged 65 years, and
lies buried in the graveyard of the old Whitechapel of the North,
Cleckheaton.   [Wright was born at Moulter Hill, Halifax.—EDITOR.]

Dialogue I.—Richard and Matthew.

ONE day, as Richard walk'd abroad
Along the fields, in thoughtful mood,
Revolving in uncertain thought,
The different schemes by preachers taught ;
The different methods of salvation
Bliss t' attain and shun damnation ;
And very wishful in his mind
The safest way to heaven to find ;
But much perplex'd and puzzled quite,
At which was wrong or which was right ;
While this affirms, and that denies,
What this calls truth, that says is lies.
Yet both their proofs bring from the Bible,

To show their scheme is justifiable,
Each wond'ring how the scriptures can
Be twisted so by any man.

As Richard slowly walk'd the plain,
And various thoughts disturb'd his brain,
He Matthew meets, a neighb'ring man;
And thus the conference began.

MATT.—How fares my friend? What thoughts employ
Your mind, or thoughts of grief or joy?
You seem indeed in thought profound,
And studious meditation drown'd.

RICH.—I think it very strange, my friend,
To hear religious folk contend
With such a fierce and bitter zeal,
About what doctrine's good or ill;
To argue, write, and preach so long,
Concerning which is right or wrong.
While each, and ev'ry one pretend
To be to sacred truth a friend,
They make that book their only rule,
Which Christians own infallible,
For guiding through life's dubious maze:
Yet they explain it fifty ways!
Churchmen, Presbyterians, Quakers,
New-lights, Independents, Shakers,
Anabaptists, Antinomians,
Methodists, and Sandimonians;
Supralapsarians, and Moravians,
Sublapsarians, and Baxterians;
Ranters, Mystics, Puritans,
Inghamites and Lutherans;
Many besides of old renown,
Not easy to be noted down,
Calvinists, Arians, and Socinians,
Pelagians, Papists, and Arminians;
Churches Greek, and Latin too,
With many more, both old and new,
Than you would think, or I can shew.

Now, my dear friend, were you to sound
These diff'rent sects in order round,
They'd every one in turn, you'd find,
Be right ; and ev'ry other blind !
And from the Bible clearly shew,
That all which they profess is true ;
And be quite positive and sure
Their doctrines are both just and pure,
That they expound the scripture right,
And set it in its genuine light ;
As if their sect above the rest,
Infallibility possest ;
As they alone deserv'd esteem,
And wisdom liv'd and dy'd with them !
" Now which are wise, and which are fools ?
" The reader's tost among those tools ;
" The more he reads, the more perplex'd,
" The comment ruining the text : "
While all these parties to derive
Their system from the Bible strive,
Most leave the genuine sense behind,
A sense more suitable to find ;
And while their learning they display
Explain the meaning quite away.

What shall a poor enquirer do,
To know what's false, and what is true ?
While diff'rent parties so much vary,
And give their judgments so contrary.
Surely 'tis possible to know
The truth of what the scriptures shew ;
Those fundamental truths at least
Which all must know, or can't be blest :
Else were we a most wretched race !
What thinks my friend upon the case ?

MATT.—Richard, completely to explain
The various points all these maintain,
Would be an endless task indeed !
Suffer me therefore to proceed,
(Waving the whims all these conceive)
To tell you, friend, what I believe.